Trapped at Sea

On their hands and knees the boys inched toward the stairs leading into the cavern. On the far wall they noticed twenty cradles containing nearly completed atom bombs.

The trigger of each bomb was already in place. Firing one of these would start a chain reaction, producing a searing, shattering nuclear detonation. Dr. Minkovitch was already assembling gleaming uranium hemispheres into spheres, one inside another. Then he fitted them into the rear compartments of the bombs.

"I hope he knows what he's doing," Frank muttered. "If one of them goes off, they'll all go. The island will disappear, and you'll be able to see the mushroom cloud from the moon!"

Suddenly a low tick-click came from the console, one per second. The Hardys looked at each other in horror. It was the countdown used in nuclear testing!

"Minkovitch must be hard of hearing!" Frank hissed. "And each second brings us closer to the bomb's detonation!"

The Hardy Boys Mystery Stories

Available from Wanderer Books

THE HARDY BOYS® MYSTERY STORIES

TRAPPED AT SEA

Franklin W. Dixon

WANDERER BOOKS
Published by Simon & Schuster, Inc.

The author wishes to thank Dr. William W. Ennis
for his expert advice on nuclear devices.

Copyright © 1982 by Simon & Schuster, Inc.
All rights reserved
including the right to reproduction
in whole or in part in any form
Published by WANDERER BOOKS
A Division of Simon & Schuster, Inc.
Simon & Schuster Building
1230 Avenue of the Americas
New York, New York, 10020

Manufactured in the United States of America
10 9 8 7 6 5 4 3 2
10 9 8 7 6 5   pbk

THE HARDY BOYS, WANDERER and colophon are
registered trademarks of Simon & Schuster, Inc.
Library of Congress Cataloging in Publication Data
Dixon, Franklin W.
Trapped at sea.
(The Hardy boys mystery stories; 75)
Summary: The Hardy brothers travel from the highways
of eastern United States to tropical islands trying to
track down truckloads of precious cargo that are being
hijacked.
[1. Mystery and detective stories]   I. Orloff,
Denis, ill.   II. Title.   III. Series: Dixon,
Franklin W. Hardy boys mystery stories; 75.
PZ.D644Ts   [Fic]   82-4793
ISBN 0-671-42362-2   AACR2
ISBN 0-671-64290-1 (pbk.)

Contents

1 *Mysterious Cargo*

Frank Hardy was driving behind a Mack truck that was traveling ten miles below the speed limit. His seventeen-year-old blond brother Joe, who was a year younger than Frank, sat in the passenger seat, and their friend Chet Morton was behind him.

"This guy's sightseeing," Joe grumbled. "Why don't you pass him, Frank?"

"I will," Frank said and started to pull out around the truck. Suddenly, without signaling, the truck driver also swung left in an effort to overtake a slow-moving farm tractor.

"Watch out!" Joe cried.

But Frank had gone too far already. He realized in an instant that even if he put on the brakes they

1

would still crash into the truck. Blasting his horn and flooring the accelerator, he moved to the left as far as he could. The road was narrow, but he had almost cleared the truck when its bumper caught the right rear wheel of the Hardys's yellow sports sedan.

"Oh, no!" Chet cried out, hiding his face behind his hands.

The boys careened ahead for several hundred feet, wildly rocking back and forth as Frank fought for control of the car. Finally, they slowed and drifted onto the right shoulder.

"I guess we're not dead?" Chet ventured after they had come to a stop.

"No," Joe said. "But it's a miracle we weren't hurt."

The boys got out and looked at the crushed rear wheel. The huge truck had pulled up behind them and the driver and his backup man walked over.

Both were lean, lanky men of middle age. One of them waved on the driver of the tractor, who had stopped out of concern.

"Sorry," the truck driver apologized. "I didn't see you pull out behind me. Are you fellows okay?"

"We're not injured," Frank said. "But our car's a mess and we're still three hundred miles away from home."

"Our insurance company will take care of the

damage," the driver assured him. He handed Frank his license number and the boy noted that his name was Jerry deToro. "This is Steve Burrows," Jerry said, indicating his backup man.

Frank introduced himself and the other two boys. Then he wrote down all the information he needed for insurance purposes.

"We can't drive our car," he said. "Could you give us a lift into the next town?"

"We'll be glad to," deToro declared. "But you'll have to ride in the trailer. There's no room in front."

"That's okay."

The trailer was loaded with refrigerators, but there was plenty of room because it was only three-fourths full. Before closing and latching the back door, Jerry cranked open a sliding panel in the roof to let in light and air. It was a warm spring day, and sun poured through the rectangular opening.

As the truck began to move, chubby Chet Morton rubbed his stomach. "We should have told him to stop at Hamburger Heaven," he said. "This experience has made me hungry."

"You'll survive," Joe said. "It's only about half an hour to the next town."

The air brakes hissed ten minutes later and the big truck came to a halt. "Get that thing out of the way!" the boys heard Jerry deToro cry.

Then a gruff voice said, "Step down, both of you. Easy now, and you won't get hurt."

Jerry's voice quavered. "Don't shoot, mister. We're coming out."

In the back of the truck, dark-haired Frank grabbed his brother's arm. "It sounds like a hijacking!"

"What'll we do?" Chet whispered anxiously. "They'll open the back door in a minute!"

Frantically, the trio looked around for a place to hide, but there was none. The refrigerators were packed solidly at the front of the trailer, strapped in place so that they wouldn't slide.

Joe looked at the vent in the roof. "Up here!" he hissed. "Hurry!"

Scrambling on top of a refrigerator, he reached out to grip the edge of the opening and pulled himself up. Then he lay on his stomach and reached inside to give Frank a hand. Finally, both of them hoisted up Chet. But the opening was not quite large enough for the plump boy, and he got stuck above his belt!

Just then they heard the back door being unlatched.

"Pull harder!" Chet urged, violently kicking his dangling feet.

Frank and Joe risked being seen by the hijackers on the ground by rising to their knees. Then they tugged with all their might, and Chet came through

4

the sky light like a cork pulled out of a bottle. Instantly, the boys flattened themselves on the roof around the opening.

The door swung open and they could see two men wearing ski masks peer into the trailer. Both of them carried pistols. One said in a pleased tone, "Refrigerators. There's at least a $10,000 profit here." Then he raised his voice and called, "Get those jokers back here."

Two more masked hijackers appeared, prodding Jerry deToro and Steve Burrows before them. The gruff-voiced man ordered the pair into the trailer. DeToro and Burrows looked surprised at not seeing the three boys there but said nothing. Obediently, they climbed in. The door was closed and latched.

The two drivers looked all around and even stood on tiptoe to peer over the tops of the refrigerators. Chet started to open his mouth, but Frank motioned him to silence. Frank thrust an arm down through the roof opening and waved to the men below. When they looked up, startled, he put a finger to his lips. Both men nodded.

The engine of a truck ahead of them started, then they began to move. The trio on the roof shifted around to face forward. Another tractor-trailer rig, this one a Kenworth, was about fifty feet ahead. It had several license plates, all coated with mud.

After a short ride, the lead truck turned off on a

dirt road. The Mack truck followed. A half-mile later the road ended at a large clearing. The Kenworth truck swung left and stopped; the Mack truck turned right and stopped. Then both of them backed up until their rear doors were only a few feet from each other.

The boys looked down and saw two masked hijackers get out from each truck. The rear doors of both vehicles were opened, boards were laid across the intervening space, and deToro and Burrows were brought out.

"Now transfer the cargo into the Kenworth!" the man with the gruff voice commanded with his hand on his pistol.

The drivers obeyed silently. When the job was finished, they were ordered into the back of the Mack truck again.

Just as they were about to climb in, Chet emitted an enormous sneeze. Frantically, all three boys pulled their heads away from the opening before any of the hijackers looked up.

"Somebody's in here!" one of the masked men exclaimed.

Quickly, Steve Burrows pulled out his handkerchief, held it over his mouth, and sneezed as loudly as Chet had.

"It was him, dummy," the gruff-voiced man grumbled. Then he slammed and latched the door.

As soon as the Kenworth truck had driven off, the boys crawled forward, dropped down onto the coupling between the cab and the trailer, and jumped to the ground. Frank unlatched the rear door to let the two drivers out.

"Boy, are we glad you managed to hide from those creeps!" Jerry deToro said in relief.

Chet put his arm around Burrows's shoulder. "Thanks for sneezing, Steve. I almost blew the whole thing."

"You couldn't help it," Steve Burrows consoled the boy. "Now let me go and call the police on the CB radio."

He disappeared into the cab, but a moment later let out a cry of disappointment. "Those crooks took the keys!"

"There's no way to start the truck or get to the radio without the ignition key," Jerry said glumly. "I guess we'll have to hike into the next town."

When the group arrived, the hijackers had a two-hour head start. Jerry deToro phoned the state police, who promised to look out for the Kenworth truck. He also phoned his employer, the Ortiz Trucking Company of Boston, to report the hijacking and have someone bring him a duplicate key.

Frank called the automobile club to have their car towed to a repair shop, then reported the accident to the insurance company in Bayport. He asked the agent to call the Hardys and the Mortons to tell them about the delay. Then the group checked into a motel.

As soon as the car was repaired, the boys returned home. Mr. Hardy met them at the front door. Tall and middle-aged, but with a youthful appearance, he had once been in the New York City Police Department but was now a private detective.

"Your mother's been worried," he said, examining the boys with his eyes for any sign of injury.

Laura Hardy, a slim, attractive woman with sparkling blue eyes, rushed down the stairs. "Were any of you hurt?" she asked anxiously.

Fenton Hardy's sister, the boys' Aunt Gertrude, came from the kitchen at that moment. The tall, angular, energetic woman with black hair gave the boys no time to reply. "So you wrecked your car," she said. "I told your father you shouldn't be gallivanting all over the countryside. Who was driving?"

"Frank," Joe said. "It was the other guy's fault, no one was hurt, and the car's now as good as new."

They all went into the front room, where the adults listened to the boys' story. When Frank described the hijacking and mentioned that the truck belonged to the Ortiz Trucking Company, Fenton Hardy exclaimed, "Another one!"

"What do you mean, Dad?" Frank asked.

"I'm going to Washington tomorrow morning to help the FBI investigate a series of hijackings from the same company. The stolen cargo all seems to vanish into thin air without leaving a clue."

"Why is the FBI involved in this type of crime?" Joe asked. "Armed robbery is a matter for the local police."

"Apparently, their interest is in one particular cargo," Mr. Hardy said. "I won't find out what until I get to Washington, because it's top secret. Would you fellows like to help?"

There were enthusiastic replies from all three boys.

"Great. Here's what you do. Drive to Boston tomorrow and report to Cy Ortiz at the Ortiz Trucking Company. I'll arrange with him for you to be put on as backup drivers. No one but he will know you're undercover operators. If necessary, you can reach me through the FBI in Washington. If I need to contact you, I'll call Cy."

"If the hijackers hit my truck, they're in for a surprise," Chet said. "I just read a book on karate." He struck a pose with his hands held in the air and yelled, "Ai-yah!"

Joe winked at his brother, then hooked his foot behind Chet's ankle and jerked. With a grunt, Chet sat down on the floor.

"You didn't yell!" he complained. "How am I supposed to know you're going to attack if you don't yell?"

Joe laughed. "Those hijackers won't yell either, Chet. We've had a brush with them already. They mean business!"

2 Narrow Escape

Aunt Gertrude invited Chet for dinner. Since she was the best cook in Bayport, the plump boy needed no urging.

"Just let me call Iola to make sure she can pick me up afterwards," he said and reached for the telephone.

"Why don't you ask her over, too?" Aunt Gertrude suggested.

Chet nodded and dialed. After a short conversation with his sister, he held his hand over the mouthpiece and said, "She can't come. Callie's visiting her."

"Callie is perfectly welcome," Aunt Gertrude assured him.

"Great." Chet spoke into the phone, then said, "They'll be here in fifteen minutes!"

"Oh, good," Frank said with a grin. Blonde, brown-eyed Callie Shaw was his girlfriend. Joe often dated Chet's vivacious, pretty sister Iola. Since they hadn't seen the girls for a while, it was a joyful reunion. Even Aunt Gertrude's dire predictions that the boys were heading for trouble by getting mixed up with criminals failed to quell the festive mood.

"Don't worry, Aunt Gertrude," Chet said. "I'll karate chop anyone who tries to jump Joe or Frank."

Iola giggled.

"What's so funny?" her plump brother asked.

"I was thinking about that board you split," Iola said. To the others she explained, "He laid a board between two wooden boxes and kept hitting it with the edge of his palm. Every time he would say, 'Ouch,' and rub his hand, but nothing happened to the board. Finally, he sat on it and it broke."

Joe grinned. "You'd better forget karate if we get in a jam, Chet. Just sit on anybody who jumps us."

Mr. Hardy said, "If you boys are going to work as backup drivers, you'll need licenses to operate eighteen-wheel rigs. I know Frank and Joe can handle them, but can you, Chet?"

"I can drive anything," Chet declared.

"Don't those big trucks have more gears than a regular car?" Callie Shaw asked.

"Sixteen," Chet replied promptly.

"So many?" Mrs. Hardy asked. "Isn't it difficult to shift?"

"Not if you know how," Chet said. "If you have trouble shifting down on a steep hill, you just double-clutch. I've driven all kinds of farm equipment, and I know I can handle those big babies without any trouble."

"All right," Mr. Hardy said. "I'll arrange for licenses for you. You can pick them up at the motor vehicle bureau in the morning."

After breakfast the next day, Frank and Joe drove their father to the airport. Before the detective said good-bye, he handed Joe a small, flat box about the size of a deck of cards.

"What's this?" Joe asked.

"A new detective kit I just put together," Mr. Hardy explained. "Read the instructions on the way to Boston."

"Thanks, Dad."

"And fellows—be careful, will you?"

"Don't worry, we will," Frank and Joe promised. Then they picked up Chet and drove to the motor vehicle bureau, where they took a written test as well as a road test to satisfy the legal requirements.

Soon they were on their way to Boston. While Frank drove, Joe read aloud the instruction booklet for the detective kit. "Hey, this is neat," he said.

"It contains a set of miniature tools, a bugging device, an electronic bug detector, and some small pellets that release red smoke when crushed and dropped on the ground."

Frank chuckled. "Smoke pellets saved our necks once before, remember?" He was referring to a tight situation they had been in in *THE MUMMY CASE*.

The Ortiz Trucking Company consisted of a huge warehouse next to a parking lot containing about twenty tractor-trailer rigs. The boys found Cy Ortiz in an office off a loading ramp. He was a tall, angular man who somewhat resembled Abe Lincoln without a beard. When the boys introduced themselves, he closed the door for privacy.

"Are all of you licensed to drive eighteen-wheelers?" he asked.

The boys produced their temporary licenses.

After examining them, Ortiz said, "You Hardy boys are too well known to work under your own names. I'll put you on as Frank and Joe Harrison."

"I'm as well known as they are," Chet said. "I've been on most of their cases with them."

Cy Ortiz looked at him. "I never heard of you."

When Chet looked wounded, Joe said diplomatically, "He's been mentioned in the news a lot. You better list him as Chet Martin. Wait a minute!" he

14

suddenly exclaimed. "Jerry deToro and Steve Burrows know who we are. This will never work."

"Don't worry about them. They're on a cross-country run to California," Ortiz assured him.

"Just what do you want us to do, Mr. Ortiz?" Frank asked.

"Find out who's been stealing my trucks! The one you boys were on the other day was the fifth hijack in the last six months. The total loss is almost a quarter of a million dollars. The police think that all the jobs are pulled by the same gang, because the *modus operandi* is always the same. Four masked men in an empty truck block the road, force my drivers into the trailer at gunpoint, then take both trucks to an isolated area to transfer the cargo. Then they lock the men in the trailer and take off."

Joe nodded. "Also, their license plates are always covered with mud."

"Right."

"According to Mr. Hardy," Chet spoke up, "the stolen cargo hasn't been traced to known fences. How do you account for that?"

"I think that the stuff is being shipped overseas, which means the gang must have a freighter."

"Mr. Ortiz," Joe said, "Dad told us that the FBI is interested in a particular cargo that was hijacked. Do you know what that was?"

"I know what it was supposed to be," the company

owner answered. "It was a shipment of boxes marked 'drill bits' from the Fargo Mining Company to a nuclear power plant in Virginia."

From the way he phrased it, the boys realized that Cy Ortiz did not believe the cargo had really been drill bits.

"What do you think was actually in the boxes?" Frank inquired.

"I have no idea," Ortiz replied. "But I don't believe the FBI would be interested in drill bits."

Chet's eyebrows shot up. "Since it was going to a nuclear power plant, could it have been nuclear material of some kind?"

"I thought of that," Cy Ortiz admitted. "But the FBI isn't talking. At any rate, the gang must have an inside contact here at the warehouse, because they seem to know when valuable cargo is being shipped." The man rose to his feet. "Come on, I'll introduce you to my foreman, Ox Manley. He'll be assigning you jobs."

They found the foreman in the warehouse, supervising the loading of steel beams onto a flatbed trailer. The beams were being lifted from a pile by a portable crane. The crane's cable ended in a magnet grip that fastened onto the steel beams so solidly that no hook was required.

Manley was a huge man with the build of a gorilla. When he saw his boss approaching, he signaled the

16

crane operator to stop. Ortiz introduced the boys, and Manley nodded with a smile.

"I want you to put them on as backups," Ortiz told the foreman.

"Do you have licenses?" Manley asked the boys.

"I've checked them," Ortiz said quickly. "They're in order."

"Are they union?"

"No," Ortiz replied. "I'll clear it with the union so they can drive pending application for membership."

Ox shrugged and said, "We may as well use them on that three-rig convoy leaving in the morning." He called to a man standing nearby. "Take over loading these beams, Sam, while I show these guys around."

Cy Ortiz headed back to his office. The man named Sam signaled for the crane operator to pick up a beam. As the magnet descended to attach itself to steel, Ox motioned for the boys to follow him.

Joe, walking between Frank and Chet, glanced up as the heavy steel beam swung over their heads. Suddenly, he realized that it was slipping from the magnetic grip! Both of his hands shot out sideways as he pushed the boys out of the way a microsecond before he himself hit the floor in a headlong dive.

Crash! There was a huge clang as the steel beam

smashed onto the concrete floor where the boys had stood only a moment before.

Ox Manley swung around as the trio climbed shakily to their feet. "You clumsy oaf!" he roared at the man on the crane. "Get down here!"

The crane operator, a thin man with a hatchet face, scrambled out of his seat. "I never touched the release button, Ox," he insisted. "There must be a short somewhere!"

"Check it out, Sam," Ox ordered. "Then get another crane operator who isn't all thumbs." To the thin man he said, "You're grounded from that crane and are back to truck driving, Ted."

"I'm sorry, Ox," Ted said.

"Don't apologize to me. Tell it to these guys you almost beaned."

"I'm really sorry, fellows," the deposed crane operator mumbled in a hoarse voice.

"Forget it," Frank said. "No one was hurt."

"Ted Herkimer here will be driving the truck with Joe in the morning," Ox Manley said quickly and introduced the boys. Then the group continued outdoors to the parking lot, where Ted showed Joe the GMC truck they would be riding in.

"And be more careful with the truck than you were with the crane," Ox warned.

Ted nodded. "I'll check it out right now to make

sure it's working okay," he said and climbed into the cab.

Manley, meanwhile, introduced the boys to the other drivers. The man Frank would back up was a dark, lean Indian named David Falcon, who drove a Freightliner truck. Chet's driver was a small, dapper man with a Cockney accent named Avery Smithson. He had a White truck.

"Everybody report at eight-thirty in the morning," Manley ordered, then went back to the warehouse. The young detectives headed for their parked car in the street.

As they neared the exit from the parking lot, they heard the growl of an engine behind them. They turned around and froze in fright.

The GMC tractor, detached from its trailer and with Ted Herkimer behind the wheel, was roaring straight at them!

3 Nighttime Search

Joe and Chet jumped one way, Frank the other, and the tractor shot between them, barely missing all three of them. Air brakes hissed, and then the vehicle came to a halt and its engine died.

Ox Manley ran back out of the warehouse and yelled, "What's the matter with you, Herkimer?"

The hatchet-faced man climbed from the cab. "The accelerator stuck," he cried, standing on the step to reach in and work the pedal with his hand. Then he came the rest of the way down and said, "It seems to be all right now. Boy, what a scare!"

"Any more accidents and you're fired," Ox said hotly. "Now get that tractor back where it belongs."

"Don't get yourself in a tizzy," Ted told him re-

21

sentfully. "I didn't do it on purpose!" He climbed back into the cab, started the engine, and backed the tractor to its trailer.

Cy Ortiz came from the warehouse to see what was going on. When Manley told him, he frowned and said, "Maybe you better let Herkimer go."

"I wish it were that easy," Manley said. "But you know it'll be a hassle with the union. We can't prove that it's him rather than equipment failure that caused these problems, and besides, he's a good driver. As soon as he does something wrong that I can prove, I'll get rid of him." With that, the foreman went back inside.

Cy Ortiz sighed and said to the boys, "He's got a point there. But I'm getting quite suspicious of Herkimer. I saw him prowling around in loft number two the other night."

"What's there?" Frank asked.

"The cargo due to go out in Herkimer's truck tomorrow—miniature television sets of a radically new design called Spectrocolor. It's an extremely valuable shipment."

Chet said, "Maybe the gang plans to steal the cargo from the warehouse this time instead of hijacking a truck."

"That's a thought," Ortiz said. "I'd better post a guard in that loft."

"You don't know which of your employees you

can trust," Joe objected. "Suppose we sleep in the loft tonight?"

"That's a good idea," Ortiz agreed. "I'll have three canvas cots set up there." He took them back inside to show them the freight elevator leading to loft number two, and gave Frank a key to the building. "I'm always the last to leave," he said. "I'll lock up around six-thirty."

"Do you want us to be here before then?" Frank asked.

"No. I'm sure the gang won't strike until well after dark, if it does at all. You fellows have dinner first and get here about eight."

The boys went to a nearby diner, then returned with a change of clothing and some toilet articles from their suitcases. They had packed these items in a small bag, and Chet was elected to carry it.

"Just remember, I expect a tip for this," he quipped when Frank unlocked the warehouse door. "A big one, too, since we have such fancy accommodations." He glumly looked at the dim night lights that were set up to illuminate the dismal room.

Joe chuckled. "The Hilton it's not, but at least we don't have to climb up to the loft. There's the elevator. Come on."

The boys soon emerged in the loft. There was no light, but they had brought flashlights. Three canvas cots were set up in one corner. Chet put the bag down near them, and they began to inspect their surroundings. Joe found a wall switch that turned on an overhead bulb, which made their task easier.

Piled near the freight elevator was the shipment of Spectrocolor miniature TV sets, crated four to a carton. Frank noticed a cardboard tag tied to the top carton by a piece of wire. Written in the corner were two small letters: AI.

"What do you suppose that means?" Frank asked the others, pointing to the letters.

Joe had no idea, but Chet quickly said, "American Indians."

The other two looked at him. "Could you explain that?" Frank asked.

"I only interpret," Chet said. "I'm not into explanations."

Suddenly, the light went out.

"W-what happened?" Chet whispered.

Frank turned on his flashlight and the others followed his example. "I don't know," he said. "Let's just be quiet and see if we hear anything."

But nothing stirred in the warehouse. After a while, Chet shifted his weight. "Maybe the breaker tripped," he offered. "I saw a breaker box next to the elevator on the first floor. I'll go down and turn it on again."

"One little bulb would hardly overload the circuit," Joe objected, but Chet had already gone to the elevator and slid open its slatted wooden gate.

Suddenly, his flashlight disappeared and Frank and Joe heard a scream of terror!

"He fell down the shaft!" Joe exclaimed.

Frantically, he and Frank rushed to the elevator and directed their flashlight beams downward. The car was on the first floor and Chet's light, still glowing, lay on its roof thirty-five feet below. About six feet down, Chet clung tightly to one of the cables.

"Hurry!" he cried. "I can't hold on much longer. My grip is weakening!"

"Just one more minute," Frank said. "We're on our way."

Joe had already flattened himself on the floor. "Grab my ankles," he said to his brother. Frank gripped him tightly, finding an anchor for his feet in the uneven floor.

Joe wriggled forward until he hung head down from the waist. His fingers touched Chet's balled fists, but he couldn't get a grip on his wrists!

"I—can't—hang on any longer!" Chet croaked.

"If you don't you'll break both legs!" Joe said sharply. "Frank, I need another four inches!"

Frank stretched as far as he could. Chet's double grip on the cable released the instant that Joe grasped his wrists, and he swung freely, his full weight now borne by Joe.

"Heave!" Joe called to Frank.

Bracing his feet, Frank pulled back on Joe's ankles. Instantly, he knew he'd never make it. Unless Chet could find a foothold somewhere, the weight would be too much for him.

"Chet—help!" Frank croaked.

Chet was moving his legs slowly and carefully so Joe wouldn't lose his grip. Finally, his feet felt an indentation in the wall, and he quickly supported his weight on it. "I found a step," he said. "There must be a series of them for the men who work in these shafts. Let me see—ah, here's the next one."

With Joe still holding his hands, Chet walked up the rest of the way. When they had pulled him to safety, all three boys lay prone in exhaustion for a few minutes, then climbed to their feet shakily.

"I thought I was a goner," Chet said. "Thanks, guys."

Joe, who still felt icy fear in all his limbs, tried to make light of the matter. "I figured we'd still need you, pal."

Frank pressed the call button and the car slowly began to rise. When its roof came level with him, he reached out to lift Chet's flashlight from it. The car continued to rise until it was even with the loft. Frank handed Chet his flashlight and all three boys focused their beams into the elevator. It was empty.

"How come it works when the lights are out?" Chet asked.

26

"Different circuits," Joe said. "But who called it down to the first floor?"

"Let's check it out," Frank said, and the three got into the elevator.

The night lights were still burning on the first floor but no one was in sight. They searched Cy Ortiz's office, the repair garage, a tool room, a storage room, and a rest room, but saw no one.

"Let's check that circuit-breaker box," Frank said tensely. "Someone must have played with the switches."

They found one of the levers in the off position. Chet turned it back on. "That ought to take care of the light in the loft," he said.

"Maybe that's where the intruder is now," Joe whispered. Cautiously, he opened the slatted wooden door to the elevator. "Hey!" he cried in a subdued voice. "The elevator *is* upstairs!"

Frank pressed the button to bring down the car. The trio silently got in and went up.

The loft was dark when they got off. They moved over to the wall switch and Joe flicked it. To their surprise, nothing happened! He directed his flashlight at the overhead bulb. It was broken!

Just then Frank spotted the silhouette of a thin figure as it moved from behind a pile of television crates toward the elevator.

27

"There he is!" Frank cried as he centered the light on the intruder and rushed toward him.

Joe and Chet followed. The stranger, startled by Frank's light beam, reversed himself and ran back behind the cartons. Frank and Joe chased after him, while Chet tried to head him off on the other side of the cargo.

A moment later there was the sound of two bodies crashing together, followed by a grunt of pain. The Hardys halted to focus their lights on the pair on the floor. *Ted Herkimer lay flat on his back with Chet seated on his stomach!*

"Get off me, you elephant," the hatchet-faced man said in a strangled voice. "I can't breathe."

Chet climbed to his feet. Herkimer got up much more slowly.

Joe grinned at his chubby friend. "I'm glad you took my advice. That was much more effective than karate." Then he turned to Herkimer. "What are you doing here?"

"That's my question to you crooks," the thin man said belligerently.

"Crooks?" Chet said with indignation. "Mr. Ortiz told us to guard the loft. You're the only unauthorized person here."

After a short silence, Herkimer said to Frank, "Is that true?"

"It's true," Frank confirmed. "We're waiting for your explanation."

The thin man said, "I was driving by and saw a light in the loft. I figured it was a burglar and came to investigate. I was headed downstairs to call the police when you jumped me."

"How'd you get in?" Joe asked.

"The warehouse door was unlocked."

Joe looked at Frank, who looked embarrassed. "I guess I forgot to relock it," Frank said.

While the boys really didn't believe Ted Herkimer's story, there was no way they could disprove it. They escorted him back downstairs and out the door. This time Frank locked it from inside.

They found a new light bulb in the storage room and took it upstairs. The three of them wrestled one of the TV crates into the center of the loft for Joe to stand on while he replaced the shattered bulb.

"I don't think any more will happen tonight," he said as he jumped down. "Let's go to bed."

However, in the middle of the night a strangled yell brought both Joe and Frank bolt upright out of sound sleep. Grabbing their flashlights from the floor alongside their cots, they focused the beams on Chet. He had kicked off his blanket and was flailing his arms and legs. Joe reached over to shake him awake.

Staring into the light, Chet asked groggily, "What happened?"

"You were having a nightmare," Joe said.

"Ohhhh," Chet groaned. "I was driving my jalopy with a huge, teetering cargo of TV sets in the back. The stack was just about to fall on my head!"

Frank chuckled. "Oh, brother. We should have let them fall. Maybe it would have shut you up!"

"Thanks, pal," Chet grumbled. But then he had to laugh. "Sorry, guys, for waking you up."

The boys were up early the next morning. They quickly dressed and headed for the elevator.

"There's a rest room downstairs where we can wash up and brush our teeth," Frank said.

As they started past the pile of TV crates, Joe suddenly came to a dead stop. "Wait a minute," he said excitedly. "You see this?"

"What?" Chet asked, suppressing a yawn.

"That tag marked 'AI' is gone!"

4 Hijacked!

"Herkimer must have taken it last night!" Frank cried out.

"This guy's definitely a suspect," Joe said. "It's too bad we can't prove anything."

"We'll watch him closely," Frank advised. "Eventually, we'll get something on him."

The boys went out for breakfast. When they came back, the warehouse was open and the three trucks of the convoy were being loaded. Ted Herkimer's GMC truck was in the warehouse, backed up to the freight elevator, and workmen were stacking the Spectrocolor TV sets inside it.

Avery Smithson was backing his White tractor into the warehouse. It was coupled to the flatbed

31

trailer containing the steel beams. Meanwhile, the Indian driver, David Falcon, was supervising the loading of his Freightliner truck outside with bales of newsprint.

"I think we should tell Cy Ortiz what happened last night," Joe suggested after a few moments.

"Right," Frank agreed. "Let's see if he's in his office."

The trucking company owner was there when the boys entered. He stared in surprise when he heard their story. "I have no idea what 'AI' means," he finally said. "And now I'm even more worried about Herkimer. His truck, by the way, is the only one you have to worry about being hijacked in this convoy."

"Why is that?" Chet asked.

"The steel beams are too heavy for the crooks to handle, and the newsprint isn't valuable enough to interest them. Perhaps I should switch Herkimer to one of the other trucks."

"No. Let's just go ahead as planned," Joe said. "I'm riding with him, and perhaps I can expose him if he's up to no good."

"Okay. But keep a sharp eye out. Those TV sets are just the kind of cargo that hijackers love."

By nine-thirty, the trucks were loaded and ready to go. Avery Smithson took the lead, with Chet riding as his backup. Dave Falcon's truck was second, with Frank riding in the passenger seat. Ted Herkimer and Joe brought up the rear in the GMC truck.

As they pulled out, Avery Smithson said to Chet, "You've got some experience with these big fellows, I 'ope, old chap?"

"I can drive anything on the road," Chet boasted.

"That's a comfort to 'ear, with a cargo like ours. We're carrying much more weight than the other chaps, you know, and a downhill runaway situation could be the end of us."

"You won't have to worry when I'm behind the wheel," Chet assured him.

Frank was getting acquainted with Dave Falcon in the Freightliner truck. The Indian told him that he was a full-blooded Iroquois and had been raised on a reservation.

Frank said, "Last night I saw a cargo tag with the letters 'AI' printed on it. Do you have any idea what it meant?"

"I never heard of it," the Indian replied with a shrug.

In the trailing White truck, Joe was asking the same question. Ted Herkimer said he didn't know what he was talking about.

"The tag was wired to one of the Spectrocolor crates," Joe said. "After you left, it was gone. We thought you must have taken it."

"Well, I didn't," the hatchet-faced man told him. "Why would I want a silly tag?"

Traffic cutting between them separated the three trucks, but they had arranged in advance to halt for lunch at a place called Barry's Truck Stop halfway between Boston and Washington. It was about one-thirty when they stopped. The six sat around a big table in the diner. They carried on an animated conversation, during which Ted Herkimer tried to convince the boys that he wished them no harm and that the previous events had simply been accidents.

When lunch was finished, everyone went outside again. Now the backup drivers took the wheels.

Joe waited for the other two trucks to pull out first, then followed.

Traffic had become even heavier than it had been that morning, and the three soon became separated. The two lead trucks were far out of sight when Joe said, "At least in all this traffic we're not likely to be hijacked."

He was not prepared for Herkimer's sharp answer: "That's what you think!"

Something in the man's voice sent a chill down Joe's spine. "What do you mean?" he asked.

"There's a dirt road a half-mile ahead. Turn right on it."

"Why should I do a silly thing like that?" Joe challenged, looking at the man.

34

"To keep from getting hurt," Herkimer replied evenly, pulling out a pistol.

"So you're the inside contact," Joe exploded. "Why are you revealing yourself?"

"Because we know who you three boys really are, Joe Hardy. I've seen your picture in the paper many times," Herkimer sneered. "We realize that your father's on to us, so we'll quit after this one. Now, the road's up ahead."

Joe slowed and geared down. He surreptitiously reached into his pocket containing the detective kit and he worked out one of the small pellets. As he swung onto the side road, he crushed it between his fingers and dropped it out the window.

About a quarter-mile along the dirt lane, they came to a deserted farmhouse with broken windows. Parked alongside it was the same Kenworth tractor-trailer rig used in the previous holdup. Herkimer made Joe back the GMC around until its rear door was close to the hijacker's truck.

Four men in ski masks got out of the Kenworth truck. Joe recognized the gruff voice of the leader as the same man who had robbed Jerry deToro's truck. Boards were again laid between the two trucks and the cargo was transferred.

As they were moving the last crate, a piece of cardboard fell from Herkimer's pocket. Joe stooped to pick it up and dropped it into his own pocket.

Herkimer did not notice. Instead, he prodded Joe into the rear of the truck. "Sweet dreams, Hardy," he sneered. "And don't forget to give our regards to your father, if you're still alive when they find you!"

With that, he locked the door. Joe felt the front being jacked up, and then the tractor drove off behind the Kenworth truck. It was apparently too valuable for the crooks to leave behind!

It was pitch dark in the trailer, but Joe felt his way to the crank to the sun roof and opened it. That let in light and air, but since there was nothing to stand on, he could not use the vent as an escape route.

I hope someone notices the red smoke, Joe thought. Then he pulled out the card Herkimer had dropped. *It was the cargo tag with the letters "AI" on it!*

Meanwhile, the two lead trucks had come to a long, gradual hill. As the faster-moving cars passed the White truck Chet was driving, Frank managed to close the distance between them until his Freightliner was just behind it. After they went over the crest of the hill and started down the steep grade on the other side, their speed increased.

"There's a bad curve at the bottom," Avery Smithson warned Chet. "And there's a fifty-foot drop behind the fence on the right. You'd better gear down a bit."

Far below, perhaps a mile and a half ahead, Chet

could see a sharp curve to the right. He started to shift down and moved into neutral. But suddenly the transmission refused to work! Racing the engine, he tried to double-clutch, but to no avail. When he tried to pull back into the previous higher gear, that also failed. The truck was locked in neutral and was gaining speed by the second. Beads of sweat formed on the boy's forehead. He was in big trouble!

"The bloody gearbox is acting up again," Avery said. "You'll 'ave to rely on the brakes, old chap."

When Chet put his foot on the brake pedal, it went clear to the floor. "We don't have any brakes!" he cried out.

"What!" Avery exclaimed. "That can't be. Try again!"

The speed rapidly increased. The speedometer registered sixty, then seventy, then eighty. Chet frantically pumped the brake pedal, but there was no air pressure at all. He blasted his horn at a slower-moving car ahead. The startled driver looked into his rear-view mirror and swung onto the shoulder just in time to avoid being smashed in the rear. The big White truck shot past.

"We'll have to jump!" Chet yelled.

"At this speed we'd be killed," Avery yelled back. "We have to ride it out."

"We'll never make that curve," Chet said in a trembling voice. "What are we going to do, Avery?"

"I suggest we pray," the little Englishman said, closing his eyes.

Behind them Frank realized what was happening and shifted the Freightliner truck into high gear. The space between the two trucks had grown to a hundred yards, but as Frank floored the accelerator, it gradually closed again. Twenty yards behind the rocketing White truck, Frank blasted his horn to warn oncoming traffic of his intention and swung left to pass. Traffic coming up the hill quickly pulled off to the side.

The White truck was now traveling at ninety miles an hour. The Freightliner truck inched past ninety-five. When the rear of the trailer was clear, Frank swung in front of the runaway truck. He kept the same speed, but the White truck's speed continued to increase. The distance from its front bumper to the Freightliner's rear decreased from twenty yards until the two gently touched.

As soon as Frank felt the pressure, he began to shift down. But slowing his own truck and holding the enormous weight of the Freightliner enough to make it around the curve seemed impossible.

Frank geared down as rapidly as he could, double-clutching when necessary. Still, the speed was far too great. Gradually, he applied his air brakes while continuing to shift down lower and lower.

He had reduced ten gears and had the brake pedal

nearly to the floor by the time they were fifty yards from the curve.

Dave Falcon said, "We're not going to make it," and braced his hands against the dashboard.

Frank felt sweat collect on his forehead and roll down into his eyes, partially blinding him. Even if they survived the crash, they could never survive the crushing weight of the steel-beam cargo that was bound to spill on top of them!

5 *Stolen Uranium*

All the way down the hill, Chet had been strug-
gling with the transmission. Now, with the speed
greatly reduced, he had meshed into one of the
lower gears. Instantly, there was a braking effect
that slowed the White truck enough to let the
Freightliner pull ahead. Relieved of the enormous
weight pushing against his rear bumper, Frank was
able to slow sufficiently to make the curve without
rolling over. Both trucks slowed, drifted over onto
the shoulder, and rumbled to a stop.

Frank and Dave Falcon climbed out, still shaking.

"That was an excellent piece of driving," the Indian commended the boy. "I'm not sure I could have
pulled it off."

Frank grinned weakly as the two walked to the other truck. Chet and Avery were just getting out of the cab.

"Whew!" Chet said, mopping his brow. "That was more exciting than the roller coaster at Disneyland!" But his trembling hands belied his carefree comment.

"What happened to your truck?" Frank asked.

"The gearbox was stuck and we 'ad no brakes," Avery replied. "Thanks for 'elping us, old chap. I'd already said my last prayers."

Dave Falcon knelt beside the tractor to examine the air-compression tank. After several moments, he rose to his feet and said, "This was no accident. An air valve was loosened!"

"I bet it was Ted Herkimer!" Chet whispered to Frank.

"He'll have some explaining to do when he and Joe get here," Frank replied grimly.

Dave Falcon, who was an expert truck mechanic, said he could fix the brake system, but it would take him at least two hours. Chet volunteered to act as his assistant.

When a half-hour passed without the third truck appearing, Frank began to worry. He decided to drive back to look for the GMC truck. He and Avery Smithson jacked up the front of the tractor and uncoupled the trailer from it, so he wouldn't have to drive with it.

Frank drove back several miles without spotting the GMC truck. Then he saw a narrow column of red smoke spiraling up from a ditch on the left side of the road. He noticed the dirt road and swung left onto it.

"What are you up to?" Avery asked.

"My brother left me a clue. It's very possible they turned into this road. Just bear with me for a little while, Avery. I have to check this out."

A quarter-mile from the main road they found the GMC trailer parked next to the abandoned farmhouse.

"Well, I'll be!" Avery exclaimed. "Do you think they got 'ijacked?"

"I'm sure of it. And I have a hunch who did it, too."

"Who?"

"Your former colleague, Ted Herkimer."

As Avery stared at him in surprise, he went behind the trailer and unlatched the door.

"Hi," Joe said. "I'm sure glad to see you!"

"I noticed your smoke signal," Frank said with a grin. "And I think I know what happened. But let's get back in the truck with Avery and you tell us on the way."

"Instead of taking the highway, go through the

next town," Joe advised. "That way we can stop at the police station."

Avery was surprised at Joe's story, while Frank just nodded. "It figures," he said.

Soon they drove up to police headquarters. The sergeant put their description of the Kenworth truck and the GMC cab on the air, along with a description of Herkimer. He made it clear to the Hardys, however, that he didn't have much hope of catching the criminals.

"They have a couple of hours lead," he said. "And there are hundreds of trucks on the roads."

Frank nodded. "May I call my company in Boston, please?"

"Sure, go ahead."

Cy Ortiz was not in, so he spoke to Ox Manley. The foreman sounded furious when he heard of Herkimer's villainy. "I should have fired him like Mr. Ortiz suggested," he stormed. "At least I'm glad we know who was behind this. I'm sure now we'll have no more trouble."

After finishing his conversation with the foreman, Frank decided they should also report the hijacking to their father. Mr. Hardy said he wanted to see both boys as soon as they got to Washington.

"Right, Dad," Frank said. "But because of the delay for brake repairs, I don't think we'll be there till tomorrow. I imagine we'll stop over some-where."

"All right," Mr. Hardy said. "When you get here, come to the Glasgow Motel. I'm in room twenty-six."

The boys drove to where the White rig and the trailer of the Freightliner were parked.

It took longer than Dave Falcon had anticipated to fix the White truck's brakes, and they weren't ready to move on until six in the evening. Since the Ortiz warehouse in Washington would be closed long before they could get there, they decided to stay overnight at a place called Orville's Trucking Oasis, fifty miles outside of Washington.

The place was crowded, and the parking area, large enough for two dozen rigs, had barely enough room for their trucks to squeeze in.

Only two rooms, both on the second floor of the two-story barracks and both with twin beds, were available.

"It looks like somebody isn't going to sleep to-night," Chet said. He looked worried.

Joe grinned, "Do you want to volunteer?"

"Ah, I'm still a little sore from my fall into the elevator shaft," Chet declared.

"All right, buddy, you can have the bed," Joe offered. "There's a sleeping bag in the Freightliner's cab behind the seats. It's not much room, but enough for me."

After dinner, Joe went outside and climbed into the truck. He took off his shoes and jacket, but left on the rest of his clothing before slipping into the narrow compartment behind the front seat.

In the middle of the night, he was awakened by the noise of metal clanking against metal just below him. He sat bolt upright, wondering if he had been dreaming. But then the noise came again.

Something strange is going on here, Joe thought as he pulled himself out from his sleeping bag. He partially eased open the cab door and stuck out his head. A shadowy figure was kneeling on the ground, using a wrench on the truck's air-compressor tank!

Joe pushed the door wide open, intending to drop on the intruder. But the unoiled hinges squeaked. The man looked up. It was so dark that his face was only a white blur. With a curse, he leaped to his feet and ran.

Joe hit the ground and rushed after the fleeing figure. He had no shoes on, however, and the gravel in the parking area hurt his feet. Forced to slow down, he watched the stranger disappear through the barracks door.

The fugitive was already running up the stairs when Joe rushed inside and hurried after him. No one was in the lobby, which was illuminated by a dim light.

On the second floor, the stranger flung open the door to Frank and Chet's room, which was the closest to the stairs. The room was dark, but Joe could see by the dim night light in the hall that the fugitive was climbing out the window.

"Wh-what's going on?" Frank asked sleepily.

Joe had no time to answer. When he reached the window, the stranger was already on the fire escape. As the young detective placed his hands on the sill to vault through, the man swung his wrench. The glint of metal warned Joe of what was coming, and he jerked back his hands just before the heavy tool smashed onto the sill.

The man spun and ran down the fire escape. Joe leaped through the window, but the grilled flooring was as hard on his tender feet as the gravel had been. He watched in frustration as the intruder dropped to the ground, ran to a parked car, and drove off.

Frank had climbed out of bed and switched on the light by the time Joe crawled back inside. Chet was still snoring gently.

"What was it?" Frank asked.

"I didn't get a look at his face, but I think it was Ted Herkimer," Joe said. "He was trying to sabotage the air compressor on the Freightliner."

47

"Oh, no! We'd better tell Avery and Dave!"

The two drivers were angry when they heard what happened, and the little Englishman decided to spend the rest of the night in his truck.

"And I'm going back to the Freightliner," Joe declared. "That way we're covered."

"That's a good idea," Frank agreed, then returned to his room, where Chet had slept through the whole thing.

In the morning, Dave Falcon checked the brake system of both trucks and found them in perfect working order. "I suppose that creep didn't have enough time to do any damage," he declared.

The trucks arrived at the warehouse of the Ortiz Trucking Company about eleven in the morning. In view of Herkimer's statement to Joe that the theft of the TV set cargo was the last the gang intended to pull, the boys, after talking to Cy Ortiz on the telephone, quit their jobs as backup drivers. Then they took a taxi to the Glasgow Motel.

Fenton Hardy answered the door at room twenty-six. Another man was with him. "This is FBI agent Stewart Zegas," the detective said after he had introduced the boys.

"We're looking forward to your report," Mr. Zegas said. "Why don't we have lunch sent in, and then you fill us in on what happened."

Over ham sandwiches, the boys told their story.

When they finished, Mr. Hardy said, "You've had quite an experience. I'm just glad you weren't hurt. Now it's time for us to bring you up to date. Stew, can you brief them?"

"All right," the FBI man agreed. "Boys, the hijacked cargo marked 'drill bits' actually was uranium. There was enough for someone who knows the technology to build many atom bombs. And we have no idea who has it."

Frank said, "If we can track down Ted Herkimer, I bet we can find it."

A slight scraping sound at the window next to the door caused everyone to look up. Through the closed curtains the silhouette of a man's head could be seen.

"Someone's eavesdropping," Mr. Hardy whispered. Then he said aloud, "Well, I guess that's it for tonight," and ended with some casual remarks about breakfast the next day.

Joe, meanwhile, had gotten up and walked to the door. He opened it a crack as Frank and Chet crowded behind him to peer over his shoulder.

No one was there now, but a familiar figure was hurrying toward the street.

"It's Ted Herkimer!" Joe whispered. "He followed us here!"

6 *The Gang's Hideout*

Herkimer jumped into a parked Ford sedan and drove off. Instantly, the three boys dashed out of the room and into the street.

An empty taxi drove past at that moment. When Chet put two fingers in his mouth and gave a piercing whistle, the taxi made a U-turn and came back. The trio jumped into the rear seat.

"Follow that green Ford," Frank ordered, pointing.

Herkimer seemed unaware that he was being tailed, because he took no evasive action. He headed east on Route 50 to Route 2, then north alongside Chesapeake Bay. After a time, he turned east again onto a narrow dirt lane.

When the taxi eased into the lane, the boys could see the green Ford parked beside two other cars by the right side of a cottage at the water's edge. They immediately instructed the driver to stop. The hijackers' Kenworth tractor-trailer and the tractor from the GMC rig stood on the opposite side of the cottage.

"We walked right into the lion's den!" Joe said under his breath.

As Frank paid the driver, Chet asked fearfully, "Shouldn't we have him wait? What if we have to run for it?"

"I spotted a roadside emergency phone about three miles back," Joe said. "We can call another taxi from there."

"Run three miles?" Chet asked in horror.

"Our football coach would say it's good for us," Joe quipped.

When the taxi had driven off, the boys cautiously moved along the lane toward the cottage. Suddenly, the door opened and Ted Herkimer stepped out. Luckily, he was talking to someone over his shoulder and failed to see them.

"Hit the dirt!" Joe hissed, throwing himself to the ground.

They watched as the hatchet-faced man went to his car, lifted a suitcase from the trunk, and re-entered the cottage.

"It looks like he's moving in," Frank said in a low voice. "I guess it's all clear."

Climbing to their feet, they approached the small house warily. At the water's edge, there was a dock with three motorboats tied to it. About fifty yards to the left stood another cottage with a dock. A twelve-foot dory with an outboard motor was moored there.

Everything was quiet. The boys walked to the front windows but found that the drapes were drawn. They put their ears to the glass but could hear nothing. Stealthily, they moved around to the side where the trucks were parked. There they found a screened window that was open.

Cautiously, the three peeked inside. Five men were seated around a table and one of them was Ted Herkimer.

A stocky, square-faced man said in a familiar gruff voice, "If Fenton Hardy is on our trail, we'd better get those Spectrocolor sets out to the ship fast."

"Don't get nervous, Mack," Herkimer said and shrugged. "Hardy and his sons will never find us here, but the Coast Guard might stop us if we try to move that cargo in daylight. We'll wait until dark."

"We could at least get the motorboats loaded," Mack suggested. "They don't have to be run out to the *Mary Malone* until tonight."

"All right," Herkimer agreed. "Unload the truck and get those cartons on the boats."

As Mack and the other three rose from the table, the boys retreated to hide in the underbrush. They watched the hijackers come from the cottage and begin carrying the Spectrocolor TV crates from the truck down to the dock, where they loaded them aboard the three boats.

Chet whispered, "When they take off at dark, we could follow them in that boat at the next cottage."

"That's a good idea," Frank whispered back. "Let's talk to the owner."

They crept through the underbrush to the other house. Its entrance was on the side facing away from the hijackers' cottage, so the boys could not be seen from there when they rapped on the door. A card on the mailbox alongside the door was lettered CALEB JONES.

A tall, bent, elderly man answered the door. "Mr. Jones?" Joe asked.

"Yep."

"Is there any chance of our renting your boat?"

The old man looked dubious. "It depends on who you young fellers are."

"I'm Joe Hardy, this is my brother Frank, and this is our friend Chet Morton."

The old man raised his eyebrows. "Joe and Frank Hardy? Not the sons of Fenton Hardy, are you?"

54

When Joe admitted that they were, Caleb Jones welcomed them with enthusiasm. "I'm a long-time fan of your pappy," he said. "You can use the boat for nothin'."

Frank said, "We appreciate that, Mr. Jones, but it wouldn't be fair. We're on a dangerous mission and might not be able to return it. Our father would compensate you if that happened, though. We'll give you our address in Bayport, so you can bill him, if necessary."

"That'll be fine," the old man said. "To seal the deal, you boys can stay for dinner."

Caleb Jones was a bachelor who lived alone, but he was a good cook. Obviously, he would have liked to know all about the case the boys were working on, but he accepted their explanation that it was confidential.

"Do you know anything about your neighbors on the right?" Frank asked.

"Nope. There's lots of traffic there, though."

"What kind of traffic?" Joe asked eagerly.

"Oh, trucks, boats, that sort of thing. And plenty of company."

Further questioning yielded no more details, however, and as soon as it got dark, the boys went to the dock and got in the dory. The outboard motor was fifty-five horsepower, which would be fast enough for them to keep up with the hijackers' motorboats if they traveled at cruising speed but not if they opened up all the way. Frank sat in the rear and started the motor. At low speed, with as little noise as possible, he moved the boat out about a hundred yards. There they drifted without running lights, waiting for the hijackers.

It was quite dark when they heard an inboard engine start. Then the running lights of one of the motorboats switched on as it pulled away from the dock.

"They've got their throttle wide open," Frank whispered. "At this rate, they'll leave us in the dust!"

"Pretty wet dust," Chet grumbled. "What'll we do?"

Just then a second set of running lights appeared far behind them.

"They're sending the boats out in intervals!" Joe exclaimed. "All we have to do is set a parallel course and we've got them!"

Frank ran another hundred yards out from shore so that the boat wouldn't spot them as it went by. By the time the second boat had passed them, a third set of lights was visible far behind them. They had now reached the mouth of the Chesapeake Bay and were in the rolling waters of the Atlantic.

"Oops," Chet said as the dory began to pitch. "I'm getting seasick."

"Then stop facing me and lean over the side," Joe advised warily.

Chet gulped and managed to control his nausea, but even in the darkness his face looked green.

Lights approached them from head-on at a distance of fifty yards and headed for shore. It was the first motorboat returning. Minutes later the second passed on its way back to the cottage.

The third boat appeared within a hundred yards, and the boys followed its lights at full throttle. Frank slowed as he spotted an anchored ship that the small boat was approaching. Shortly afterward he cut the gas until the motor was barely idling, and they drifted to within fifty yards of the ship.

The boat was tied up alongside. By the glow of its mooring lights, the boys could make out the name *Mary Malone* on the bow of the ship.

"Hey, they're lifting stuff aboard with a crane," Chet whispered. "What do you suppose it is?"

"Spectrocolor TV sets—" Joe began but was interrupted by the whine of a windlass spinning out of control. There was a large splash followed by a curse.

"You lost one of the crates, you idiot!" a voice bellowed.

"Something's wrong with the windlass," the crane operator cried. There was a short pause, and then he added, "Cog's busted. It'll take me an hour to replace it."

"You got anyone to help you?"

"No. The crew's still in town for dinner. They won't be back for a while."

"All right. We're going back, too. I don't think it's a good idea to hang around here for an hour. We'll see you later."

As the motorboat chugged off toward shore, Frank put his hand on Joe's arm. "If we could get a look at the ship's log, we could learn its destination!"

Joe blinked. "We'd have to go aboard to do that."

"That's what I had in mind."

"Are you crazy!" Chet exploded. "There are a bunch of crooks on that ship!"

"Most of them are in town, remember? I think we have a good chance to sneak aboard without anyone noticing us." Frank twisted the throttle of the dory enough to get to the opposite side of the ship, away from the crane. When he spotted a hanging rope ladder, he cut the engine and drifted close enough for Joe to grab it.

Joe tied the dory to the rope ladder, then swung himself out of the little boat. When he was halfway up, he glanced down.

Frank was talking to Chet. "Maybe you'd better stay here and wait for us," he suggested.

Chet, who was still not feeling well, gave him a

withering look. "No way. I'm coming with you."

"Okay. Let's go." Frank moved up the ladder. Chet climbed to his feet, swayed back and forth, and nearly fell overboard before grabbing the rope ladder to steady himself. Uttering a groan of despair, he began to climb.

When the trio had almost reached the top, Joe suddenly stopped dead. He had heard a noise! Then a voice just above him said sardonically, "Welcome aboard!"

7 Trapped!

A chill went down Joe's spine as he slowly looked up. But, to his relief, there was no one in sight!

Then he heard Ted Herkimer say, "I'm sailing with you to Atlantic Island, captain. I've got to get out of the country because the Hardy boys know I'm a member of the gang."

"Are you coming along, too, Larsoni?" the captain inquired.

Mack responded in his gruff voice. "Yeah. Ted says there'll be no more hijacking for a while because Fenton Hardy and the FBI are hot on our trail."

"Is this the last cargo, then?"

"Yes," Mack Larsoni replied. "As soon as you finish loading all the stuff, you can hoist anchor."

"That'll be a while," the captain said. "Come below and I'll show you your quarters."

There were receding footsteps and the sound of a hatch cover opening and closing. Joe climbed the rest of the way up the ladder and peered over the rail. He saw the crane operator on the opposite side of the ship, but no one was close by. Cautiously, Joe climbed over the rail and motioned for the others to follow.

As they crouched next to a lifeboat, Frank whispered, "We don't need to see the log now. Herkimer said they're going to Atlantic Island."

"I'll bet that's what 'AI' on that tag meant," Chet said. "Atlantic Island. The gang marked the cargo they intended to hijack with the letters indicating their destination." After a pause he asked, "Where is Atlantic Island?"

"It's near the Bahamas," Joe replied.

"Let's take a look at the cargo," Frank suggested, "so we can describe it to the police, then get out of here."

"Good idea," Joe said.

They crept forward to the same hatch through which the captain and the two hoods had disappeared. The ladder led to a corridor running forward and aft on the deck below. A number of cabins were on each side, and through the open door of one of them the boys heard the voices of the captain, Herkimer, and Mack Larsoni.

Joe cautiously led the way aft. Coming to another hatch, they peered into a mess with an attached galley. It was empty. Farther aft they looked into an engine room where an engineer was examining gauges.

Silently, the trio walked along a side corridor to the port side of the ship and found the hatch to the cargo hold. Since there were no workers on this level, the young detectives peered down into the lighted freight compartment.

It was nearly filled with crates and bales. The boys recognized refrigerators and Spectrocolor television sets by the type of boxes they were in. Other things apparently were from prior hijackings.

"I think we've seen enough," Chet whispered. "Let's get out of here now."

The boys retreated the way they had come. As they reached the mess room hatch, Herkimer, Mack Larsoni, and a bulky, graying man wearing a gold-braided cap came from the forward cabin with the open door. Quickly, the trio ducked into the mess room until the three men disappeared up the forward hatch to topside.

After a few moments of silence, the boys emerged and continued on. As they descended the ladder and stuck their heads out of the upper hatch, they noticed the three men on the rail on the opposite side of the ship.

"Phone the boss and tell him we've sailed," the captain called down to the pilot of the motorboat.

"Okay," came the reply.

"I wish he'd mention who the boss is," Joe whispered.

Frank nodded. "Well, let's get out of here."

The boys went the rest of the way up on deck and crept along the starboard rail to the rope ladder. The sea had become rougher during the time they'd been aboard, and the ship was rolling badly. A large wave swept the dory against its side, and they could see the rope snap. The dory floated a dozen yards away.

"Now what?" Chet asked anxiously.

"We'll have to swim for it," Joe replied.

"In this storm? We'll drown!"

Then another wave drove the dory into the side of the *Mary Malone*. It filled with water and sank.

Chet's white face became ashen. "Wh-what are we going to do now?"

"We'd better find a place to hide," Frank said tensely.

"It looks like we're going to Atlantic Island," Joe said. "For free, too!" He tried to sound cheerful but his voice was strangled.

At that moment, the men at the opposite rail

headed for the hatch, and the boys ducked beneath the lifeboat.

As soon as the trio had disappeared below, Frank, Joe, and Chet crossed the deck to port side. The loading hatch had been closed and locked, but they knew there had to be access to the hold somewhere by means of a ladder. They found it forward of the loading hatch and descended two decks into the hold.

"If this is where we have to spend our time, I'll forego the free trip," Chet complained.

"There's no choice," Joe whispered and turned on his pencil flashlight, since the lights had been switched off. "Now let's check out this stuff and find a spot for ourselves."

Silently, they moved along the aisles formed by the stacked crates and bales. Against the port bulkhead, roped firmly in place, were the refrigerators hijacked from Jerry deToro's truck. Markings on other crates indicated they contained electric typewriters, computer equipment, home appliances, oriental rugs, and fur coats.

"There's a fortune in stolen goods here," Joe said in awe.

"I'd settle for a blanket and a nice dark hole," Chet declared.

"Let's see what's aft," Frank suggested.

They found a small alcove about eight feet square formed by boxes piled on three sides.

"This is cozy enough," Frank said. "Now if we could get some of those fur coats to sit on—"

However, the rugs and coats were baled with strap iron that would require bolt cutters to shear.

"I'm afraid it's the bare floor," Joe said.

"How long will it take to get to Atlantic Island?" Chet asked.

"Oh, it's about twelve hundred miles," Frank replied. "How fast do you figure this tub can travel, Joe?"

"Twenty-two knots, maybe. But I doubt that it will cruise at more than sixteen to eighteen."

Frank did some mental arithmetic. "Two to three days."

"How do we eat?" Chet inquired.

"Can't you go a couple of days without anything?" Joe asked.

Chet looked horrified. "You must be kidding!"

"We can probably sneak some food from the galley," Frank said. "The safest time to raid it will be in the middle of the night. We'll let you have a midnight snack."

"If I survive that long," Chet said glumly.

A short time later they heard the anchor being hoisted and the ship getting underway. The boys sat in their alcove in the dark and conferred in low tones.

"I wish we had some light," Chet complained. "It's going to get boring sitting like this for three days."

Listening to the sound of the engines, Joe said, "I think we're moving faster than I guessed. Maybe we'll make it in two days."

Suddenly, the lights in the hold went on. The boys looked at each other in alarm, and then Joe got up and peeked into the aisle.

Drawing back his head, he whispered, "It's Ted Herkimer coming this way!"

Chet had an inspiration. "Up there!" he whispered and pointed to the top of the crates. Stooping and forming a stirrup with his hands, he motioned for Joe to put his foot in it. When Joe complied, Chet straightened to boost him upward. Joe slid onto the top of the crates on his stomach.

Chet quickly boosted Frank up, too, and then Joe and Frank reached down to grip the plump boy's hands and pull him up. They made it just in time. All three were on their stomachs, peering over the edge of the crates, when the hatchet-faced man rounded the corner.

Herkimer had a grease marking pencil in his hand. After using it on several of the crates in the alcove, he stepped back into the aisle. The boys watched him retreat to the ladder and ascend it. Then the lights went out.

The young detectives dropped down again, and Joe and Frank shone their pencil flashlights on the crates Herkimer had marked. There was a large "U" on each.

"What's that mean?" Chet asked.

"There's an Ulster Island in the Atlantic group," Frank said. "Maybe these crates are intended for there."

"Then it would say 'UI,' " Joe objected.

"What's that stamped on the crates?" Chet asked, pointing to some printing only faintly visible.

Joe shifted the beam of his flashlight.

" 'Fargo Mining Company,' " Frank read. "And look what it says here underneath: 'drill bits'!"

"I bet it's the uranium!" Joe exclaimed. "That's what the 'U' stands for. We found the cargo the FBI wants!"

8 Get the Hardys!

At midnight, the boys left the hold to make the raid on the galley. No one was in the corridor of the middle deck and they reached the mess hall without incident. Everything was dark.

"Put on your flashlight," Chet whispered.

Joe lit the way across the mess to the galley. The two rooms were only separated by a counter, however, so the light could be seen from the corridor.

"Chet, stand guard in a spot where you can see anyone approaching along the hall!" Joe urged.

"But I want to see what food there is!" Chet objected.

"Shall we throw him overboard?" Joe asked Frank in exasperation.

"I'm going, I'm going," Chet said, moving back into the mess.

There was a roast beef, a butt of ham, and a large cheese in the refrigerator. In a cabinet there were several loaves of bread. They took a sharp butcher knife, made a dozen sandwiches, and wrapped them in wax paper that they found in a drawer. Then they put the sandwiches in a paper bag and cleaned up all evidence that they had been there.

"It probably won't fool the cook if he keeps a proper inventory," Joe commented. "He'll know the food's missing."

Frank shrugged. "How about something to drink?"

Joe shone his light around and lifted a two-quart juice bottle with a screw top from the garbage. He quickly washed it out and filled it with water.

Just then Chet hurried into the galley. "Hide!" he whispered. "Someone's coming!"

Joe switched off his light and all three ducked under the counter. A moment later the light went on in the galley. Peering over the counter, the boys saw two crewmen standing inside.

"Cookie will raise Cain if any food is missing," one said in an apprehensive tone. "You know how he is!"

"He won't know who took it," the other man said. "I'm hungry."

He started toward the galley, and was almost there

70

when his friend at the door called urgently, "Somebody's coming," and switched off the light.

Both men hurried out into the corridor. The boys heard the ship's captain say, "What were you men doing in the galley?"

"Cookie asked us to check to make sure no one was filching food, sir," one of the sailors improvised. "Everything's okay."

"Oh," the captain said. "Carry on." A moment later his footsteps could be heard going one way, the two crewmen's the other. The boys retreated into the hold, carrying their sandwiches.

Chet wanted to have a feast as soon as they got back to their alcove. Joe warned, "There's four sandwiches apiece, and we won't go after more until tomorrow night. You can eat them anytime you want to, but you're not getting any of ours."

Chet, contemplating possible future starvation, settled for snacking on only half of a sandwich. Joe and Frank had none.

They spent an uncomfortable night sleeping on the floor. About five in the morning, they sneaked above to wash up in the head before any of the crewmen got up and returned to the hold without being detected. They breakfasted on a sandwich each and spent a boring day interrupted only by lunch and dinner.

At midnight, they sneaked another trip upstairs.

As they peeked around the corner into the corridor where the galley was, they saw the same pair whose raid had been interrupted by the captain the night before.

As the crewmen turned on the light in the mess, a gloating voice said, "Aha, I caught you crooks!"

"We just looked in to see if everything was all right, Cookie," one of the crewmen defended himself.

"You looked in to see what food you could steal!" the cook screamed. "You're the ones who raided the galley last night."

"No way, Cookie. Not us!" the men protested.

"Get back to bed," the cook ordered. "If I catch you around here again except at mealtime, I'll use a cleaver on you."

The two men hurried outside. The cook, a gangling man with an angry face, emerged from the mess to watch them walk away, then switched off the light, crossed the corridor, and entered a cabin. After his door closed, the boys tiptoed through the mess into the galley.

"Wow, that was a close call," Chet whispered. "He could have caught *us* instead of them!"

"That's right," Frank said. "We owe those guys our lives!"

"And if we take any more food," Joe added, "we'll get them into trouble again."

72

Chet looked alarmed. "You mean, we have to starve?"

"Let's just take a little of each," Frank suggested, "so the cook won't notice."

The small amount of food they took was sufficient, since the ship docked about eleven o'clock the next morning.

When they realized from the sounds above them and from the cessation of the engine's throb that the ship had docked, the boys crept up to the middle deck. Apparently, everyone was on top, because they saw no one. From the sounds above they could tell that the port side of the *Mary Malone* was against the dock. Figuring that most of the crew would be on that side, they ascended a starboard ladder.

They reached the top deck without being detected, but immediately heard footsteps approaching from the stern. They ducked beneath a lifeboat.

Two pairs of legs stopped in front of them.

"What I like about Atlantic Island is that any cargo will bring a good price without questions being asked," Mack Larsoni said.

"That's why the boss picked it," Ted Herkimer told him.

"Tell me something," Larsoni asked curiously. "Who actually is the big boss?"

"You'll stay healthy longer if you don't ask questions," Herkimer replied in a cold voice.

That brought a moment of silence. Then Mack spoke up. "Who's that coming aboard?"

"Just the port inspectors," Herkimer said. "Don't let them worry you. They've been paid off."

The two crossed the deck to the other side of the ship. After peering in both directions and seeing no one else on the starboard side, the boys emerged from beneath the lifeboat. Joe, for the first time, noticed a paper sack that Chet was carrying.

"What's that?" he asked.

"The two sandwiches we didn't eat. You didn't expect me to leave them, did you?"

The hatch over the hold had been opened and the crew was unloading the cargo onto the dock.

Joe asked, "How do we get off this tub?"

"Let's play it cool and just walk off," Frank suggested.

Casually, they strolled across the deck toward the gangplank, but then ducked behind some boxes when they saw Ted Herkimer, Mack Larsoni, and one of the port inspectors conversing ahead of them.

The gruff-voiced Larsoni said, "No, those crates marked 'U' don't stay here, inspector. They're going to Pirate's Port."

"Whatever you say, señor," the inspector said and walked down the gangplank to the dock.

Herkimer went over to the loading hatch to watch

the crates being lifted through it onto the dock, which put his back to the gangplank.

"Let's go," Frank whispered.

The three resumed their casual stroll. After a few moments, a burly loading foreman walked past them, stopped, and regarded them suspiciously.

"Who are you?" he asked.

"Port inspectors," Joe said and brushed past him. Frank and Chet followed.

The foreman shrugged and moved on.

They weren't afraid of being seen by Mack Larsoni, because he had never seen them before. As they went past him, he looked them over but made no move to stop them, probably assuming that the loading foreman had checked them out.

The boys went down the gangplank unhurriedly. At the bottom, a uniformed port security officer was posted.

Holding up his hand, he said, "Identification, please."

"I'm running an important errand for the port commander," Chet said quickly and pointed to his paper bag. "These two are my bodyguards to make sure I get there without delay."

"Oh," the uniformed man said, convinced that the paper bag held the payoff. "Go ahead."

Suddenly, Ted Herkimer's voice sounded from behind them. "It's the Hardys! Get them!"

9 *Parachute Jump*

"Run!" Joe cried.

It was over fifty yards from the edge of the dock to a row of warehouses, with nothing but open space between them. As Herkimer, Larsoni, and the crew members dashed down the gangplank after the boys, four stevedores, alerted by Herkimer's shout, came from one of the warehouses and closed in from the other direction.

The stevedores obviously had never played football. Joe stiff-armed the lead man out of the way. Frank threw a body block into another, rolled clear as the man went down, bounced to his feet, and raced on. Chet simply ran into the other two as they converged on him and sent them sprawling.

77

The contact cost Chet, too. The paper sack he was carrying burst and spread bread, meat, and cheese in all directions.

Chet was puffing like a locomotive as they neared the warehouses. "Let's hide instead of run," he gasped.

Joe nodded and led the way through the open truck door from which the stevedores had come. There was another open door on the far side, but the boys slowed to look around. To their left was a row of square cardboard cartons and some washing machines. Apparently, the men had been packing the washing machines in the cartons when they were interrupted, because some of the cartons had machines in them and others were empty.

Joe turned one of the empty cartons on its side, with the open end facing away, and climbed in. Frank and Chet quickly followed suit. They were just about settled when they heard a dozen pairs of feet race by.

Joe took out a pocketknife to carve a small hole in the right side of the carton. Putting his eye to it, he saw the band of pursuers standing just outside the far doorway, looking in all directions.

Then they came inside again. When they neared the overturned cartons, Ted Herkimer said to Mack Larsoni, "They must have had a car waiting, which probably means Fenton Hardy is here, too."

"So what?" the gruff-voiced Larsoni said. "Even if he brought FBI agents with him, they have no jurisdiction on Atlantic Island."

"Nevertheless, they can make plenty of trouble for us," Herkimer declared. "If they show up again, I want them grabbed."

Eventually, Herkimer, Larsoni, and the other crew members headed back for the ship, and the four stevedores returned to work. Three of them lifted a washing machine while the fourth reached for what was supposed to be an empty carton.

When it didn't budge, he said in a surprised voice, "This is already loaded."

Quickly, Chet shot out, grabbed the man, threw him down, and sat on him. As the three others dropped the washing machine to rush at him, Joe and Frank crawled from their cartons and thrust their legs in front of two of them. The pair tripped and fell, but the fourth threw himself at Chet.

The plump boy rolled onto his back, causing a grunt of pain from the man he was sitting on. He drew his knees up to his chest and placed his feet into his attacker's stomach. As the stevedore fell atop him, Chet grabbed his shirt and at the same instant straightened his legs. The man made a back somersault in the air and landed on his back with the wind knocked out of him.

79

The other two stevedores jumped to their feet. One swung at Frank, who ducked and drove a fist into the man's stomach. It was like hitting a board. The man didn't even grunt. He swung a left and Frank ducked again. The boy backed away, parrying blows or ducking as his attacker bore in with flailing arms, strong as an ox but totally unskilled at boxing.

Finally, Frank snaked in a left jab that threw his opponent off balance, followed by a smashing right to the jaw. The man's arms dropped to his sides, he swayed on his feet, and then crashed onto his back.

Meantime Joe's opponent landed a lucky right that knocked Joe down. The man attempted to kick him in the head, but Joe rolled aside, bounced to his feet, and delivered a series of blows to the man's stomach and face. A hard one-two to the jaw ended the fight. His opponent sat down heavily, his eyes crossed, and then he rolled over on his side.

Chet got up from the man he was sitting on, but the prone stevedore made no attempt to rise. Instead, he gasped for breath. The boys ran for the far door of the warehouse. A half block beyond, streetcar tracks made a circle and headed back the other way. A streetcar was parked in the circle. As they climbed aboard, Joe asked the conductor where they could find a hotel.

"The Atlantic is a good one and we go right by

it," the man told him. "I'll let you know when to get off."

Ten stops later the conductor called, "Carson Street, Atlantic Hotel."

The hotel was in the center of a shopping area. The boys bought fresh clothes before registering, so that they could shower and change. There was a bank nearby, and, since they might run into considerable expense, Frank used his credit card to draw five hundred dollars.

A suave, sleekly dressed desk clerk made a supercilious sniff at their rumpled appearance as they registered.

Chet said, "You would look messy, too, mister, if you'd slept in a ship's hold for two nights in your clothes."

"I must admit that I've never done that," the clerk said haughtily.

He assigned them a room on the fourth floor with two double beds and a cot. After cleaning up and changing clothes, the boys discussed their next move. They decided to call Fenton Hardy in Washington and ask for his advice. When Frank picked up the phone, the suave voice of the desk clerk answered.

"Give me an outside line, please," Frank said.

"I'll place your call, sir."

"Okay. Get me FBI headquarters in Washington, DC."

After a short pause, the clerk said, "Sorry, sir, but the local police have forbidden all cable calls without a police permit."

When Frank hung up and relayed this information, Chet exploded with anger. "I don't believe it. That guy is in with the crooks!"

"There's an easy way to find out," Joe declared. "Let's go to the police."

They went downstairs and asked the desk clerk for directions to the police station. When they learned it was only two blocks away, they walked.

Oddly, the desk sergeant seemed to be expecting them. He sent them into the office of a handsome, Latin-looking captain. He rose and introduced himself as Luis Sanchez and asked what he could do for them.

Frank said, "I just tried to place a call to the United States, and the clerk at our hotel said we needed police permission."

"Yes, that is our policy," Captain Sanchez confirmed. He sat down and asked, "Who do you wish to call?"

"My father."

The captain raised an eyebrow. "The hotel clerk said that you asked for the FBI."

"He called here?" Frank asked.

"Of course. All telephone and switchboard operators are required to report attempts to phone outside the island."

"Why?" Joe asked.

"Government policy."

Frank asked, "Can I get a permit?"

"Perhaps, if your passport is in order."

The boys looked at each other, suddenly realizing they were aliens without passports in a strange land, which could mean serious trouble or even jail!

Frank said, "I left it at the hotel. The call isn't that important anyway. I guess we'll forget it."

When they got outside, Joe said, "That passport bluff was just to shut us up. The captain doesn't want trouble with influential American citizens but he does want us out of his hair."

Frank nodded. "Obviously, the police here are hand-in-glove with the crooks. What do we do now?"

"How about lunch?" Chet suggested. He pointed to a taco stand. "There's a place."

They ate tacos at an outdoor table while they discussed their next move.

Joe said, "Remember Mack Larsoni telling that port inspector that the crates marked 'U' were going to Pirate's Port? Maybe we should go there, too."

"Where's Pirate's Port?" Chet inquired.

"It's a small island some distance away from here," Frank explained. "We'll have to fly there."

When they finished eating, they got back on the street car and asked the conductor where the airport was.

"Take this line to the opposite end," he advised.

The boys thanked him but decided to go back to the hotel first to get their things. When the trio reached the small airfield, they asked the information clerk when the next flight to Pirate's Port was leaving.

"The day after tomorrow," was the reply. "There are only two flights a week."

"Oh, no!" Chet said. "Is there any other way to get there?"

"You could charter a plane."

"Where?"

"Just go out the door into the field and you'll see a hangar about a hundred yards to the right. The sign on its roof says ATLANTIC ISLAND CHARTER SERVICE."

There was only one plane in the hangar, a World War II B-24. A lean, hard-faced man in a flight suit was checking its tires. He straightened to look at the boys as they approached.

"Are you the charter pilot?" Frank asked.

The lean man nodded. "Tom Fredericks. People call me Freddie. Where do you want to go?"

"Pirate's Port."

84

"Fifty dollars each," Freddie said.

Frank paid him and the pilot told them to climb aboard. He put on a helmet and goggles, started the engine, and taxied from the hangar.

Joe asked, "How long will the flight take?"

"About an hour," Freddie replied.

The plane took off with a roar. When they were airborne, the pilot asked, "What's your business on Pirate's Port, gentlemen?"

"We're just seeing the sights," Chet told him.

"Tourists?"

"That's right."

"There's nothing much to see at Pirate's Port," Freddie said. "Corsair City is the only town of any size, and it's dead. I'd be glad to fly you to any of the other islands, though."

"No, thanks," Joe said. "We want to see Pirate's Port. Maybe we'll go somewhere else later."

The plane climbed to ten thousand feet. Suddenly, one of the engines missed, and then its propeller stopped. The craft went into a steep dive. Freddie worked the controls furiously and managed to pull out at five thousand feet, but then a second engine sputtered and died.

In a panicky voice the pilot said, "We're going to crash! Put on those parachutes in the rack over your heads and get ready to jump!"

The boys looked down. Nothing but water could

be seen in any direction, and it was probably shark infested!

Chet started to reach for a parachute, his face ashen. But Frank had sized up the situation and put a hand on his friend's shoulder. "Don't," he whispered. "The guy's bluffing!"

10 Indian Disguise

Freddie did not hear what Frank said, but apparently he realized that the boys were not doing what he had asked them to do. He turned around.

"Why aren't you putting on your parachutes?" he screamed.

"Because we know better," Frank said. "We're pilots, too. That was an impressive feathering job, but this plane can run on one engine. Don't try to feed us to the sharks!"

The pilot scowled, faced forward again, restarted the two engines, and began to wing in a wide circle.

"Where do you think you're going?" Joe demanded.

"Back to Atlantic Island. If you want to go to Pirate's Port, you can swim," Freddie sneered.

Chet, feeling less terror and realizing that Freddie was part of the gang they were after, was thinking quickly. "I'll give you thirty seconds to get back on course," he told the pilot. "If you haven't by then, I'll pull you out of there and sit on you while one of the Hardys takes over."

"If you do, I'll have you arrested for air piracy."

"No, you won't," Frank said. "You accepted one hundred and fifty dollars to fly us to Pirate's Port. If we have to take over, we'll have *you* arrested for fraud when we land!"

Chet said, "Fifteen seconds."

The plane swung back in the direction of Pirate's Port. When they landed, the pilot taxied over to the terminal, waited until the boys got out, then immediately took off again.

Watching the B-24 climb, Chet said, "We should have had him arrested for trying to make us jump."

"I'm not sure it would have done us any good," Frank said morosely. "Chances are the gang owns this place, too."

"When we left the hotel, the clerk must have alerted his buddies to follow us to the airport." Joe deduced. "Either he paid off the pilot, or Freddie's a bona fide member of the group."

"One thing's for sure," Chet said. "We're not safe anywhere."

"There's nothing we can do about that except to be careful," Frank said. "Let's take a cab into Corsair City and find a hotel."

Their driver took them to a small, neat place called the Ascot. It was only two blocks away from the waterfront. After checking in, the young detectives held a conference.

"The first order of business is to find out when the *Mary Malone* is due in," Joe suggested. He called the port authority. When he hung up, he said, "Not until nine in the morning. That gives us time to make plans."

"What we'll have to do," Frank said, "is to watch them unload the uranium, then follow it to its destination."

"The only problem is," Joe spoke up, "they know we're here, so they're going to be on the lookout for us."

"The answer is disguises," Chet declared. "We can dress up as natives. This place is filled with Indians, so who would notice three more?"

"That's a great idea," Joe said. "Let's go out and get some things before Freddie and his crew arrive."

The trio left their room and looked for an appropriate clothing shop. What Chet had said was true. At least half of the people on the street were Carib

Indians in native dress. Many of the men had machetes thrust into their waist sashes, indicating that they were laborers in the cane fields. Others wore more colorful costumes decorated with bright beads.

Near the hotel they spotted a sign on a store window: MIGUEL'S CLOTHING STORE. Miguel turned out to be a huge, bearded man with the fierce look of a pirate. When the boys told him they were invited to a costume party and wanted to go as native islanders, he produced three outfits.

Frank's clothes consisted of white trousers, a white shirt richly embroidered with colored beads, and a beaded headband. Joe's outfit was similar, but he had fewer beads on his jacket and the headband was plain. Chet was outfitted as a field worker in a simple shirt and pants and a red waist scarf. Black wigs cut with bangs and sandals went with each costume.

Miguel directed the three to dressing booths to try on their clothes. Chet had just gotten into his when the door was flung open and the fierce-looking Miguel strode in flourishing a machete!

Chet backed away from him but hit the wall after a couple of steps. As he flung out his hands defensively, Miguel dropped the weapon. "This is for you," he said in his deep voice. "It belongs with your costume." Relieved, Chet accepted the long-bladed knife.

When everyone was satisfied with the fit of the

clothes, the boys put on their own things and left the shop. They bought brown makeup on the way back to the hotel, then dropped off their purchases and spent the evening sightseeing in Corsair City.

At eight-thirty in the morning, disguised as Indians, the young detectives went to the dock. They noted a number of tough-looking characters searching the faces of all the people there.

"I bet they were hired by the gang to pick us out of the crowd," Chet whispered.

Joe nodded. "Of course, they have to rely on descriptions. I hope our disguises fool our friend Ted Herkimer as well."

"We'll know soon," Frank said. "Here comes the *Mary Malone* now."

When the ship had docked, Herkimer walked down the gangplank, conferred with one of the tough-looking characters, then strolled around the dock, checking people out. Finally, he returned to the ship.

"It worked!" Chet said gleefully.

At that moment, a hulking, pale-skinned bald man came along and addressed a group of six Carib Indians standing nearby. "Are you the dock crew for the *Mary Malone*?"

"Yes," one of the Indians replied.

"Is this all the dock office sent me?" the bald man complained. "I asked for nine!"

91

Frank whispered to Chet, "Here's your chance to get a close look at the cargo. Go over and tell him the dock office sent you."

"You'd better come with me!" Chet protested.

"We're not dressed like laborers," Frank said. "They'd be suspicious of us."

Giving them a disgusted look, Chet went to report to the bald foreman.

Frank and Joe watched from a distance as the ship was unloaded, but Chet had a closeup view. His job was to help load cargo on trucks as it was swung down to the dock by crane. It was hard work, and he put out less and less effort after a while until the foreman frowned at him.

Finally, the cargo was unloaded. The crates labeled "U" were lowered to the dock and heaved onto a two-and-a-half-ton truck. Ted Herkimer and Mack Larsoni came down the gangplank and Mack climbed behind the wheel.

"I'll be at Devil's Point if you want to contact me," he said before he drove off.

Herkimer nodded and returned aboard. Just then the foreman came over to Chet. "If you slow down anymore, you'll be in a coma. What's the matter, you don't like the job?"

Chet winced. "My back," he mumbled. "It's sore."

"Do you want to quit?"

Chet nodded.

"All right. Pick up your pay at the dock office tomorrow morning."

Chet nodded again, then turned and walked up to his friends. As he approached them, he whispered, "Is he gone or is he still watching?"

"He went back to the ship," Frank said. "What happened?"

"Larsoni drove off with the uranium. He told Herkimer he was going to Devil's Point."

"Let's rent a car and follow him!" Joe said excitedly. "There's a rental place down the street from the hotel!"

The three quickly went back to their room to change their clothes, then continued on to the agency where they rented a small Ford.

"Can you tell us where Devil's Point is?" Frank asked the clerk.

"It's on the opposite side of the island," the man replied, "Here, let me show you." He produced a map and pointed. "Only one person lives there," he explained. "Some crazy scientist who conducts weird experiments. The natives say he practices voodoo."

The boys thanked the man and drove off along the road he had indicated. It finally ended at a ten-foot iron gate with a sign on it: KEEP OUT!

"Now what?" Chet asked.

"We park in the bushes and advance on foot,"

Frank said and turned the car around. He drove fifty yards back into a narrow side lane he had spotted before and left the little Ford in a secluded spot.

The young detectives walked to the iron gate and climbed over in order to avoid making it creak.

A driveway with thick shrubbery on either side led to a large, rambling wooden house perched on the edge of a cliff. When they neared it, the boys faded into the underbrush and crept closer.

The two-and-a-half-ton truck was parked behind the house, and a pair of large, muscular men were unloading the crates and pushing them through what looked like a coal-bin chute. They finished a few moments later and went inside through a back door.

The boys made a circuit of the house. On the far side they found an open basement window and peered in. They saw a laboratory with no one in it.

"Chet, you stay here and stand watch," Frank whispered. "Joe and I'll climb in and have a look around."

Chet nodded. "If you're not back in fifteen minutes, I'll get in the car and get the police. Suppose, though, they're in with the crooks as well?"

"You'll have to take that chance," Frank commented grimly. "Come on, Joe!"

The Hardy boys climbed through the window. They wondered what the strange-looking equipment in the lab was for, until Frank stopped in front of a huge, egg-shaped device suspended in a cradle. A chill ran down his spine. "The crazy scientist is building a bomb of some sort!" he whispered.

"Let's plant a bug," Joe suggested. "Then we can eavesdrop." Quickly, he took out his tiny detective kit, extracted an electronic listening device, and fixed it beneath the workbench. Just then a door opened at the top of the stairs!

The boys scrambled out the window and eased the frame closed behind them. Peering back inside, they watched Mack Larsoni and a short, fuzzy-haired man with glasses descend the steps. Joe pulled a receiver set from the detective kit and he, Frank, and Chet put the earpieces into their ears.

"Well, Dr. Minkovitch, what do you think?" Larsoni said.

"What you brought me will complete my work," the fuzzy-haired man replied. "The bomb will be finished in a few days."

"What are you going to do with it?" Larsoni asked.

"My colleagues and I have a market—a liberation movement in Europe."

Larsoni shrugged. "That's far enough away so we won't hear the explosion. Let's settle the financial part of the deal."

"Certainly." Dr. Minkovitch went to a wall safe and took out several bundles of money. When he handed them to Larsoni, the hijacker carefully counted them before stuffing them into his pockets.

"I guess that closes the deal, doc," he said. "Pleasant explosions."

He went upstairs, and moments later drove off in the truck. As it disappeared, a sleek sports car drove up. The boys peeked around the corner and saw the desk clerk from the Atlantic Hotel step out and go into the house!

Quickly, they retreated to the lab window. A moment later, the clerk came downstairs and Dr. Minkovitch greeted him as Mr. Lanky.

"I saw Larsoni drive out," Lanky said. "He delivered the goods?"

"Yes."

"Does he know what you'll use it for?"

"He thinks it's just *one* bomb for a European liberation group," Minkovitch replied. "He has no idea that we have enough devices to plant at least one in every major city throughout the world." He sighed and rubbed his hands. "The nuclear fallout would be so disastrous that governments will surrender to us peacefully, and we'll soon rule the whole world!"

11 Atomic Scare

Beads of sweat collected on Chet's forehead. "He—he's talking about atomic bombs!" the boy whispered. "That's what he needed the uranium for!"

Frank grabbed his arm. "Shh!"

"What do you mean by 'we,' doctor?" Lanky asked in a cold voice.

"Well, won't we?" Minkovitch asked.

"The other directors and I will, not you. You're just a paid employee."

"But you can't do anything without me," the scientist said petulantly.

"True, and you will be rewarded with both wealth and prestige. Perhaps you will be given a position in the world cabinet, but get it out of your head that

97

you will help rule." Lanky's voice rose and his eyes flashed with a look of insanity. "Rule will be divided among the three directors who furnished all the money for your experiments."

"I've worked hard, Mr. Lanky," Dr. Minkovitch complained. "I deserve more than a cabinet post."

Lanky said harshly, "You speak of hard work, doctor? We could have lived like kings on our hijacking profits, but instead we slaved in menial jobs in order to pour all the money into this project. By the way, where is the uranium?"

Dr. Minkovitch led him to a door at the rear of the lab, and the two went into the storage room into which the crates had been unloaded through a chute. That took them beyond the range of the bug.

"These guys are mad!" Joe said under his breath. "We must stop them!"

Frank nodded. "But let's not leave yet. Perhaps we'll learn more."

A few moments later, the pair came back into the laboratory and Lanky asked how soon the bombs would be ready.

"They're complete except for the uranium," the doctor said.

"I see only one assembled," Lanky remarked, indicating the device suspended in the cradle.

"I do only the experimental work here, Mr. Lanky.

The dangerous assembly is done underground in what I call my factory."

"Is it nearby, doctor?"

"Near enough so that it will take only a short time to move the uranium there. I may as well take care of that right now."

The doctor switched on an intercom and said into it, "Hagar and Quark, come to the laboratory, please."

The two big, muscular men who had unloaded the truck appeared presently. Minkovitch instructed them to move the uranium to the factory. One walked into the room where the material was stored, and the other went back up the stairs.

"There is a chute with a conveyor belt from the storage room to the underground factory," Minkovitch explained to Lanky. "Hagar will go down to lift the crates off the belt as Quark sends them along."

A few moments later, the doctor and Lanky went upstairs. The boys removed the listening devices from their ears and hid in the underbrush. Soon they saw Hagar come from the house and walk toward the cliff. They were about to follow when Dr. Minkovitch and Lanky stepped out on the porch.

"I didn't know you had neighbors," Lanky said to Minkovitch.

"Neighbors? What do you mean?"

"Doesn't someone live up that lane about fifty yards beyond the gate?"

"No, of course not. Why?"

"I saw a car parked there when I came in."

"What!" Dr. Minkovitch exclaimed. "That means somebody's spying, maybe the police! Can you fix the police?"

"Not on Pirate's Port," Lanky said. "On Atlantic Island, we have them eating out of our hand, but the cops here are honest. It probably isn't them, anyway. We have word that the Hardy boys are on the island."

"Hardy boys? What Hardy boys?"

"They're the sons of Fenton Hardy, the famous private detective. You must have heard of him."

"Fenton Hardy!" the doctor said in horror. "Of course, I've heard of him. Who hasn't? Why wasn't I informed he is after me?"

"He isn't here," Lanky said in a soothing voice. "Only his two sons, Frank and Joe, plus a friend of theirs named Chet Morton. Hagar and Quark ought to be able to handle them."

"We must find out whose car it is at once," Dr. Minkovitch declared. "Of course, we do get hunters out here quite often. It could be one of them."

The two men went back into the house. Instantly, the boys jumped up.

"We have to head them off!" Joe urged.

Frank nodded. "You and Chet go. I want to see where Hagar went. I'll meet you here later."

100

Nodding, Joe and Chet slipped away while Frank hurried in the direction the big man had taken. The young detective walked through the trees edging the cliff for some distance but found no sign of the criminal.

Reversing direction, Frank reached the edge of the tree area just in time to see Hagar climb the porch steps and enter the house. How did I miss him? the boy asked himself. There must be a secret entrance to the underground factory. Apparently, I went right past it.

Joe and Chet, meanwhile, had made their way to the gate and climbed over it. Under cover of the trees, they ran to their car. Joe drove it further along the lane until he came to a small clearing. With their pocket knives, the boys cut underbrush and camouflaged the small Ford so that it could not be detected from the lane.

Then they carefully sneaked back to where the car had been parked. Dr. Minkovitch and Lanky were standing there.

"I'm telling you, this is the place," Lanky said, pointing at the ground. "See the tire marks?"

The doctor squatted down. "Yes. It must have been hunters."

The two men went back to the lane. Chet and Joe waited several minutes before following. When they finally reached the gate, Minkovitch and Lanky were just disappearing into the house. The boys climbed over the gate and joined Frank.

"Mission accomplished," Joe reported. "They think the car belonged to hunters."

"Good," Frank said. "I haven't found the entrance to the underground factory yet, but since everyone is in the house now, we can wait and follow them when they leave."

Joe nodded. "Let's see if they're in the lab."

However, when the boys came to the lab window and peered in, they saw no one. Cautiously, they made a circuit around the house, looking in other windows. On the far side they saw an open window through which they could hear voices. From the conversation, they deduced that Lanky, the doctor, and his oversized assistants were having lunch.

A miserable expression formed on Chet's face as he looked at his watch. It was twelve-thirty.

"You should have saved those sandwiches from the *Mary Malone*!" Joe teased him.

"They saved our lives!" Chet murmured. "Or maybe just prolonged them a little if we don't get something to eat soon!"

Frank put his finger to his lips and the three listened.

"After lunch, Hagar, Quark, and I will start loading the bombs," Minkovitch said. "Will you be returning to town, Mr. Lanky?"

"No, I'll wait to see how long it takes, so I can report to the other directors."

Frank motioned for Joe and Chet to follow him out of earshot.

"Joe and I'll trail Minkovitch and his goons," he said. "Chet, you stay here and keep an eye on the house."

"I've got to play watchdog again?" Chet complained. "Why can't I be in on the action for a change?"

"It'll be dangerous," Joe pointed out. "If we don't come back when they do, it means we're prisoners in their bomb factory. In that case, get the police as fast as you can!"

When Chet realized that the underground reconnaissance was, indeed, extremely risky, he nodded in relief. "Sure, guys," he said. "You can count on me!"

12 Devil's Point

The boys went back around the house to conceal themselves in the underbrush near the laboratory window. In a few minutes, Dr. Minkovitch, Hagar, and Quark came out and headed for the stand of trees edging the cliff. As soon as they had disappeared, Joe and Frank followed. Chet stayed at his post.

After a time, he grew tired of lying on his stomach in the underbrush and crawled over to peer into the laboratory. It was empty. Chet was about to push open the window to climb to the top of the stairs and listen for what Lanky was doing, when he heard the front door open and close. Hurriedly, he returned to the underbrush as Lanky went down the front steps. Then there was silence.

When Lanky didn't appear around the corner of the house, Chet crept forward to peek past the edge of the porch.

He heard Lanky's voice from the sports car. On his hands and knees, the boy crawled over to crouch behind it.

"Mohawk red calling Apache blue," the criminal said. "Come in, Apache blue."

He's talking on a car radio, Chet said to himself. Then a voice that sounded familiar, but that he couldn't quite place, replied, "Apache blue here."

"Luis, it's Lanky calling from the 'A' project site," Lanky said.

It's Captain Luis Sanchez of the Atlantic Island Police! Chet thought.

"How's it going?" Sanchez inquired.

"Doc's completing the process right now. He'll be ready to deliver on time."

"Fine. Any problems?"

"A couple of minor ones. Doc's getting a little too big for his boots. He wants equal status with the directors."

"Tell him he can have it."

"What?" Lanky said indignantly.

"Once we're in the driver's seat and don't need

106

him anymore, we can dump him. In the meantime, let's keep him happy."

Obviously, Sanchez was one of the other directors, Chet thought.

"What's your other minor problem?" the captain asked.

"I spotted a car parked near here with a rental sticker on it. It's gone now. It was probably just hunters, but it could have been the Hardy boys and their friend. Any leads on them?"

"Not since Freddie Fredericks reported that he flew them to Pirate's Port. Didn't Herkimer and his guys check them out?"

"I haven't heard but I'll inquire. Over and out."

A moment later, Lanky's voice came again. "Mohawk red to the *Mary Malone.* Come in, *Mary Malone.*"

"*Mary Malone* here," a voice said from the radio receiver.

"Ted Herkimer, please."

"Hold on."

There was silence for a couple of minutes, then the hatchet-faced man's voice said, "Herkimer here."

"Lanky calling from Devil's Point. Any word on the Hardy boys?"

"No. They definitely weren't on the dock when we pulled in. I had a team patrolling the place and they never spotted those kids."

"Then you think it's unlikely that they're around here?" Lanky asked.

"Oh, they're around all right. My guess is that they're lying low because they know we're after them."

"Well, I spotted a rented car nearby. It was probably just hunters, but I'd like to know for sure."

"How could they find the 'A' site? I think they're either hiding or have taken the first shuttle flight to Miami. Captain Sanchez gave them a good scare about their passports."

"Yeah, I guess," Lanky said, but he sounded unconvinced. "Why don't you make sure by having someone check the passenger lists of recent flights? I would rest easier."

"Will do," Herkimer said. "Anything else?"

Chet could not understand Lanky's mumbled reply, but when he heard no more talk for a few moments, he assumed that the communication was over. He began to crawl back toward the corner of the house. However, he wasn't quite fast enough.

The car door slammed and Lanky shouted sharply, "Hold it right there!"

Chet looked over his shoulder into the bore of a gun barrel! Sheepishly, he climbed to his feet.

The doctor and his two assistants were still in sight when Joe and Frank reached the cliff. The three men walked along the edge, but moments later suddenly disappeared.

Astonished, the Hardys rushed over to the spot. They noticed a path along a narrow ledge no more than two feet wide! Joe started down, with Frank right behind him.

It was a treacherous walk. A gusting wind almost blew them off the trail. They knew that one wrong step would send them hurtling a hundred feet down the sheer precipice into a raging surf breaking in huge waves against its side.

They rested for a moment. "Now I know why this place is called Devil's Point," Joe said into his brother's ear.

Frank nodded and stared into the vicious whirlpool below them.

They watched a fishing scow sailing in too close. Suddenly, it got caught in the undertow of the maelstrom. Its engines roared a frantic song of terror as its two occupants tried to fight the pull of the crosscurrents. But the boat was inexorably drawn nearer and nearer to a watery grave.

"They're going to crash!" Joe cried out. But suddenly the boat made slight headway instead of being pulled ashore. It moved farther and farther away from the furiously spinning cone of water until it finally tore free and sped off.

The boys continued down, moving carefully

and holding on to whatever support they could find.

"I suppose this gets easier with practice," Joe declared. "Apparently, it doesn't bother the doctor, and he's a lot older than us."

"I don't plan on getting any more practice," his brother said dryly.

They reached a turn, and when they peeked around the corner, they could see where the trail ended at a flat ledge about twenty feet wide. The doctor and his assistants were approaching a heap of brush piled against the side of the cliff. Hagar grabbed a branch and pulled on it, and a large wooden door swung open! After the criminals had disappeared through it, it closed behind them, erasing all signs of its existence.

Frank and Joe continued down to the ledge. Joe gripped the same branch Hagar had, and, with his heart beating wildly, eased the door open an inch. Fervently, he hoped no one would be on the other side!

No one was, and they peered into a dark tunnel with light at its far end. Joe opened the door wider and they went in.

Cautiously, they made their way along the tunnel. It opened into an enormous cavern illuminated by overhead lights. Its roof was a dozen feet above the tunnel, and the floor was a dozen feet below. The room was circular, with a diameter of a couple of hundred feet.

The boys inched on their hands and knees toward the stairs leading into the cavern. On the far wall they noticed twenty cradles like the one in the laboratory, containing nearly completed atom bombs. The trigger of each bomb, an explosive-initiated nuclear generator of neutrons and enormous pressures, was already in place near its chamber at the small end. Firing one of these would start a chain reaction that would spread to the rear compartment, which was going to be packed with more uranium. Its fission would then produce a searing, shattering nuclear detonation.

Behind the bomb cradles were racks of electronic chassis with a bewildering array of instruments and switches. A number of crates were stacked quite a distance apart from each other on the right. A conveyor belt end protruded from a narrow tunnel in the side wall.

The boys realized with horror that the crates must contain the active nuclear material because of the room in between them. They knew that if a large quantity of uranium was stored in too small an area, the mass might go critical. This chain reaction would not result in an explosion, but every living thing in the cave would be doomed by the deadly radiation.

111

The left side of the cavern contained a fully equipped laboratory and electronics shop. In the center stood several machines including lathes, milling machines, a planer, drill presses, automatic screw machines, a hoist, welding equipment, and an induction furnace.

Hagar and Quark were carrying the crates to the row of bombs, where Dr. Minkovitch was already assembling gleaming uranium hemispheres into spheres, one inside another. Then he fitted them into the rear compartments of the bombs.

"I hope he knows what he's doing," Frank muttered in a barely audible voice. "All of the initiators are already in place. If one of them accidentally goes off, it'll act as a trigger for the rest, and they'll all go. The island will disappear and you'll be able to see the mushroom cloud from the moon!"

Dr. Minkovitch finished loading the sixth bomb. As he moved on to the seventh, his elbow momentarily caught a wire extending from the cradle of the sixth bomb to the control and test console standing behind it.

Suddenly, a low tick-click came from the console, once per second. Minkovitch seemed oblivious to it, and Hagar and Quark were too far away to hear it. But the Hardys looked at each other in horror. They had heard that monotonous, cold tick-click before. It was the countdown used in nuclear testing!

"Minkovitch must be hard of hearing!" Frank hissed. "And each second brings us closer to the bomb's detonation!"

13 Chet Grabs a Crook

"What'll we—" Joe started to ask, but Frank did not hear him out. He leaped to his feet and ran down the stone steps. Hagar and Quark turned to watch in astonishment as the boy raced toward the ticking bomb.

"It started to count down when you got tangled up in the wires!" he yelled at Minkovitch. "What shall I do?"

The doctor stared at him with his eyes bulging. He cocked his head and now seemed to hear the tick-click, too, since all color drained from his face. "Depress the detonator control transfer switch!" he cried hoarsely.

Frank saw the tip of a slender lever at one end

of a slot in the initiator cover plate. He wasn't sure that it was the transfer switch and hesitated momentarily.

"Yes, that's the one!" Minkovitch hissed. "Push it!"

With trembling hands, Frank pressed the lever and held his finger on it.

"Now what?" he asked.

"Keep holding it down," the scientist replied.

Hagar and Quark approached and stared belligerently at the Hardy boy. "Who's this guy?" Hagar asked. "And where'd he come from?"

"Just be quiet!" Dr. Minkovitch said impatiently. Then he turned to Frank. "Young man, I don't know who you are, either, but you have just saved us all. Please keep that lever depressed. If you release it, the device will go off."

Hagar and Quark turned pale. "Let's get out of here!" Quark shrieked.

"You stay where you are and shut up!" Minkovitch told him. "There's nowhere on the island you'd be safe if the device goes off. The whole place and everything on it will disintegrate into random atoms. Do you understand?"

Quark trembled. "Yes, sir."

"Hagar, bring me a large screwdriver," the doctor commanded.

"Yes, sir," the big man said and brought one from

the workbench. As he handed it to the doctor, Minkovitch addressed Frank. "Now listen carefully, young man. I'm going to attempt to disarm the device. It's not complicated—all I have to do is unscrew the detonator. However, when I start doing that, control may automatically be transferred to the internal timer, and the countdown may resume. We may hear ticking again, but from the device itself this time. If we do, eh, don't worry."

"Doesn't it mean that—"

"Of course, it does," the doctor put in, "but it won't help to worry. Depending on how far the countdown has advanced, control may not have been transferred to the internal timer. Even if it has, I may get the detonator off before zero is reached. Or, possibly, I may not."

Frank stared at him.

The doctor shrugged. "Well, since there's nothing either of us can do to alter the countdown, it's useless to worry, right?"

Frank nodded weakly. Joe, from a distance, could see the hair bristle on the necks of Hagar and Quark.

"Ready, young man?" Dr. Minkovitch asked.

"Ready," Frank replied.

"Hold your thumb firm." The scientist put the blade of the screwdriver into a small hole near the initiator end and, using the tool as a lever, exerted counterclockwise pressure. A round inner section—

the detonator itself—moved slightly and the ticking began again, louder than before.

"Oh, my, it is quite advanced," the doctor said, spinning the detonator as rapidly as he could.

The ticking kept getting louder. Sweat dripped from Minkovitch's face. Frank's throat felt dry, and Hagar and Quark seemed rooted to the spot where they stood.

Suddenly, the detonator came off in Minkovitch's hands. "Thank goodness!" he shouted as the ticking stopped.

Frank released the lever and let out a breath of relief. The doctor put the detonator and the screwdriver down on a workbench, and his two assistants came to life again.

"What about this guy, doc?" Hagar asked, scowling at Frank.

"Who are you, young man, and how did you get here?" Dr. Minkovitch demanded.

"I'm just a tourist passing by," Frank replied.

"Your name?"

"John Smith."

"I'll bet he's one of the Hardy boys!" Quark declared.

"Mr. Lanky knows what they look like," Dr. Minkovitch said. "Let's take this young fellow upstairs."

The two big men grabbed Frank by the arms. Just then Joe ran down into the machine shop area. Un-

118

noticed by the three criminals, he grabbed a three-quarter-inch drill bit, stepped behind Dr. Minkovitch, and pressed the butt end of the drill into the man's back.

"Don't move!" Joe said quietly, as the doctor stiffened.

Hagar and Quark whirled around at the sound of his voice.

"Th—there's a gun in my back," Dr. Minkovitch quavered. "Please do whatever the gentleman says."

"That's sensible of you," Joe said. "Now release my brother."

Hagar and Quark released their grips.

"Okay, put your hands behind you," Joe went on. "Frank, find something to tie them up with."

There was a coil of rope next to the hoist. Frank cut three lengths and lashed the men's wrists behind their backs. Joe bound the doctor's hands, then tossed the drill bit back on the bench.

"He didn't even have a gun!" Hagar cried in an outraged voice.

"How are we going to get these guys up to the house?" Joe asked his brother. "We can't walk them along the path. They'd fall off."

Frank moved over to the conveyor belt and gazed up into the tunnel. "This is wide enough," he declared. "If the belt goes in both directions, we can use it." He studied the switch and saw that turning it to the left would make the belt move upward.

"You ride up first," he said to Joe. "Then I'll send our friends up to you."

Joe crawled onto the belt on his stomach and Frank threw the switch. It was a long, eerie ride through total darkness. Because the storage room at the upper end was as dark as the chute, he wasn't prepared for the sudden ending of the belt and tumbled headfirst onto the floor. He thrust out his hands in time to break his fall and was only a little shaken instead of injured.

In the darkness, he felt his way to the door to the laboratory and peeked inside. When he saw that the room was empty, he pulled the door open wide to let in light.

Returning to the still-moving conveyor belt, he called down the chute, "Okay, Frank."

Frank sent up Dr. Minkovitch first. When the doctor reached the top, Joe grabbed him beneath the shoulders and heaved him off the belt. It required considerably more effort to do the same with Hagar and Quark, but he managed. As Frank reached the top, Joe switched off the belt and let him climb off by himself.

There was no lock on the storage room door, but there was a hasp on its outside. They locked the three prisoners in by thrusting a screwdriver they found in the lab through the loop of the hasp.

Frank opened the basement window and called out softly. "Chet?"

There was no answer.

Quietly, the boys ascended the stairs and eased open the door at the top. It led to the central part of a long, narrow hallway running the length of the house. No one was in sight.

Cautiously, they went to the front, looking into a study, a dining room, and a kitchen. They found Chet seated at the table with a glass of milk before him, eating an enormous sandwich.

"Hi, guys," he said cheerily. "Want some lunch?"

14 Prisoners at Sea

"What happened to Lanky?" Frank asked his friend.

"He pulled a gun on me," Chet said. "But I managed to knock it from his hand and grab him. He's resting comfortably in the trunk of his car out front."

Joe chuckled. "Good for you, buddy!"

"What'd you find in the crazy doctor's toy factory?"

"Not toys, I'm afraid," Frank said gravely. "There were atom bombs, all right. But we've got the crooks locked up."

"Terrific." Chet beamed. "Now guess what."

"What?"

"Captain Luis Sanchez is one of the directors of this outfit." Quickly, Chet told the Hardys about the radiotelephone conversation between Lanky and Sanchez.

Joe whistled. "It doesn't totally surprise me."

"Right," Chet agreed. "Now tell me, what'll we do with those creeps we caught?"

"Turn them over to the Pirate's Port police," Frank suggested. "Joe and I will take Minkovitch and his two goons in our Ford. Chet, you follow with Lanky in his sports car, okay?"

"Sure thing."

Soon they were on their way to Corsair City with Joe leading the way. They had only driven a quarter-mile when they noticed a pickup truck approaching them. Suddenly, it swung sideways to block the road!

Both Joe and Chet stomped on the brakes as Ted Herkimer and Mack Larsoni jumped from the cab of the truck. Four more hoods appeared from the back!

"Uh-oh," Joe mumbled. "I don't like the two-to-one odds!" Gunning the rented Ford in a U-turn, he roared back the other way. Chet swung the sports car right behind him. Quickly, Herkimer and Larsoni jumped back into the pickup and took off in pursuit.

Just before the road dead-ended at the iron gate, Joe turned onto the narrow dirt lane and sped past the spot where they had hidden their car. The pickup was close behind them.

"I hope this'll take us back to the main road," Joe said between clenched teeth as they tore along the rutted path.

Frank merely nodded.

Their hopes were soon dashed when they realized that they were nearing Devil's Point. There the lane curved to run alongside the very edge of the cliff before suddenly ending at a barbed-wire fence.

Joe slammed on the brakes and he and Frank jumped out. Chet skidded to a halt behind the Ford. As the pickup stopped with a screech, all three scaled over the fence like Olympic champions. They saw Dr. Minkovitch's rambling wooden house ahead and realized that the fence edged his property. They were right back where they had started!

They also suddenly realized that their adversaries had dropped off four of their gang because they knew where the lane ended. Now those four were advancing from the direction of the gate. The boys were trapped!

"There's only Herkimer and Larsoni behind us!" Joe panted. "Let's backtrack!"

They turned and started toward the fence but then stopped short in dismay. Herkimer and Larsoni had freed the prisoners, and now the assault force numbered six!

Desperately, the young detectives turned again, but their four pursuers closed in to meet them. They were all big, powerfully built men. Both sides swung fists. The boys effectively blocked blows and got in some good counterpunches of their own but were steadily driven toward the edge of the cliff. Larsoni, Hagar, and Quark rushed up to join the fray. Dr. Minkovitch, Herkimer, and Lanky stayed back to watch.

With seven against three, the boys had all they could do to parry blows and no longer even attempted counterpunching. They backed up farther and farther.

At the very edge of the precipice, Chet glanced over his shoulder into the swirling whirlpool a hundred feet below. A blow to his jaw knocked him backward. He lost balance and his arms flailed helplessly as he started to pitch over the edge.

Joe and Frank grabbed him by either arm and hurled him forward. Chet crashed into two of the hoods and knocked them down, but they immediately bounced up and pinned him to the ground. The other five swarmed over Joe and Frank.

Flat on their backs with their arms and legs pinned, the two brothers looked up into the faces of Herkimer and Lanky.

"All right," Frank said. "We give up. Call off your pet apes."

The ropes that the boys had used to tie up Dr. Minkovitch, Hagar, and Quark were now used on them. When all three had their hands bound behind them, they were marched back to the barbed-wire fence. Two of the hoods held up the bottom strand so that the boys could wriggle under it on their stomachs.

Dr. Minkovitch, Hagar, and Quark returned to the house. Lanky got into his sports car and the four men who had come in the pickup climbed into the boys' rented Ford. The young detectives were loaded into the back of the truck, with Mack Larsoni holding a gun on them. Ted Herkimer got behind the pickup's wheel and led the way to Corsair City.

Frank said to Larsoni, "What do you expect to accomplish by kidnapping us?"

"I just work here," the man said in his gruff voice. "Ask the boss."

Over his shoulder, Herkimer said, "What we've accomplished is shutting you three up, not to mention rescuing our four colleagues that *you* kidnapped."

"Arrested," Joe corrected. "We were taking them to the police. I doubt that's where you're taking us."

"Oh, but you're wrong," Herkimer said with a snicker.

"You're taking us to the police?" Frank asked in surprise.

"Eventually."

The single word sounded sinister. None of the boys asked for elaboration.

After a long silence, Chet spoke up. "What brought you barreling out here, Herkimer? You must have been expecting us, or you wouldn't have brought along such an army."

The hatchet-faced man snickered again. "Lanky radioed me that a rented car was parked near Dr. Minkovitch's house. There's only one car-rental agency in Corsair City. I checked and found a Ford had been taken out by a Frank Hardy."

The young detectives winced.

"What are we going to do with these guys, Ted?" Larsoni asked.

"First we'll stick them in the hold of the *Mary Malone.*"

"Then what?"

"You heard what I told them. We're turning them over to the police."

"Were you serious?" Larsoni asked in a startled voice. "When they talk, *we'll* be arrested."

"Not the Pirate's Port police, Mack. When we get back to Atlantic Island. They haven't any passports, you know, and I'm sure Captain Sanchez can dream up enough other charges to keep them in jail for a long time."

The boys looked at each other, all of them thinking

128

of stories they had heard of Americans being arrested on trumped-up charges in Central and South American countries, sometimes languishing in jail for years!

When they reached Corsair City, Larsoni spread a handkerchief over the gun in his lap so that it wouldn't be spotted by passing motorists. The three-vehicle convoy drove to the dock and parked next to the *Mary Malone*'s gangplank.

As everyone got out, Herkimer said to Larsoni, "Run their car back to the agency, will you?" Then he turned to the four hoods who had been riding in the Ford. "Take these snoopers aboard and lock 'em in the hold."

As the boys were herded up the gangplank, they heard Lanky's voice behind them. "I'm going to fly to Atlantic Island soon, Ted. I have to get back to my job."

The three youths were taken into the empty cargo compartment. Their captors made sure their hands were tied securely behind their backs, and then they went out the hatch again. "Have a good trip!" one of them sneered before slamming the door after him.

Chet grunted. "What a break!" he said. "For all we know, they'll dump us in the middle of the ocean!"

15 Turmoil on the Dock

"At least they left the light on so we can see what we're doing," Joe said. "Frank, back up against me."

He picked at his brother's bonds until he loosened the knot. As soon as Frank was free, he untied Joe and Chet.

"Those crooks aren't very bright," Joe said. "They might have known we could free each other as soon as we were left alone."

"What good does it do us?" Chet asked. "We still can't get out of here."

"Don't give up so easily," Joe advised him.

He looked around. There was a single porthole on either side, high up near the ceiling, but the glass was painted over with black enamel so that no

131

outside light could get into the hold. The portholes were about fifteen feet from the deck, and there was nothing in the empty hold to stand on.

Joe had an idea, though. "Remember that acrobatic act we saw at the circus?" he said. "The three brothers who stood on each other's shoulders?"

"The Gimlet brothers," Chet said.

"Uh-huh. You're the one on the bottom. Stand over here."

He positioned Chet below the starboard porthole and had him face the bulkhead. First Chet stooped, made a stirrup with his hands, and told Frank to put his foot into it. When he hoisted him up, the older Hardy stepped onto Chet's shoulders.

"Now comes the ticklish part," Joe said. "I'm going to have to crawl up both your frames." He climbed up Chet's back until his feet were on the plump boy's shoulders alongside Frank's. Chet grunted at the extra weight but made no complaint.

Joe climbed Frank's back until he was standing on his shoulders. That brought his chest about even with the porthole. He unlatched it and pulled it open. Cautiously, he leaned out, looking in all directions. There was nothing on either side or below, but just above was the rail of the middle deck.

Joe pulled his head back in. "Coming down," he told Frank and Chet. He descended, and then his brother jumped off Chet's shoulders.

"The middle deck rail's just above the porthole," Joe reported. "Look for some hook we can use to pull ourselves up."

All three searched eagerly, until Chet called after a few moments, "Will this do?"

He held up a large, three-pronged hook used for gaffing fish.

"Perfect," Joe exclaimed gleefully.

He picked up the three pieces of rope that had bound their wrists and tied them together with carrick-bend knots. This gave him a rope about seven feet long, to which he tied the three-pronged gaff.

"Now we wait until dark," he said.

Chet creased his forehead. "Tell me something. How's the guy on the bottom going to get out?"

"He isn't," Joe said.

"That's what I figured. Now, you don't expect me to—"

"Look, Chet, you wouldn't fit through the porthole anyway," Joe said. "Once we're out, we'll come and open the hatch for you, okay?"

"You'll get out the easy way," Frank added. "No acrobatics. You won't have to risk your neck on the rope."

Chet considered this for a moment and objected no further. "Do you think we'll get any dinner?" he asked.

"I hope not," Frank said. "All we need is someone to come in and check our ropes!"

But either their captors had forgotten them or they were indifferent to their hunger, since no one brought any food. Chet's stomach grumbled but he kept quiet about it. Finally, he pointed to the open porthole. "It's dark out now. Can we start this rescue operation?"

Joe got up and said, "Up against the wall, you two."

He got up on Frank's shoulders again. He leaned out of the opening and cast the hook upward. It took him a while before one of the barbs caught on the rail. After testing the line, Joe pulled himself through the porthole until his legs were dangling inside.

"Now what?" Frank asked.

"Grab my ankles and climb up my legs until you can get a hold on the porthole."

Frank did and was soon hanging from the opening. Joe shinnied up the rope to the deck above. Then the older boy pulled himself through the porthole, grabbed the rope, and followed Joe up the rope.

When they had reached the deck, they crouched next to the same lifeboat as the first time they had come aboard and looked in all directions. No one was on the starboard side, but on the port side, next to the dock, they could see two crewmen guarding the gangplank and several others leaning on the rail.

"What now?" Frank asked.

"I got us this far," Joe said. "It's your turn to have a brainstorm."

After thinking a minute, Frank asked, "Do you have any idea where the ship's radio is?"

"Probably on the bridge," Joe said. "Want to go look?"

"Yep."

"Shall we get Chet first?"

Frank shook his head. "We'll have a better chance of not being detected if it's just the two of us. We'll pick him up later."

They crept forward and up a short ladder to peer into the wheelhouse. Against its starboard side they could see the panel of a shortwave radio and a ship-to-shore telephone. Seated before the panel was a radio operator, and across the cabin, looking out a port window at the dock, was the officer of the watch.

The boys backed down and crouched next to the ladder for a conference.

Frank whispered, "I'll get them out of there, and then you go in and call the police."

"How are you going to get them out?" Joe asked.

"I have a plan but no time to explain. Just watch."

Joe ducked beneath the ladder. Frank climbed up again, this time openly, and stepped onto the bridge.

"Evening, gentlemen," he said.

The radio operator looked up and the officer swung around.

"Who are you?" he demanded.

"Frank Hardy."

The officer of the watch looked incredulous. "How'd you get out of the hold?"

"Magic. I'm taking over the ship."

"You're what?"

"I'm taking over the ship," Frank said impatiently. "Get the captain up here at once."

"Are you crazy?"

Frank drew himself up to his full height. "Say 'sir' when you speak to me, sailor."

The man said to the radio operator, "This guy is nuts. Let's grab him."

The radio operator got to his feet and both started for Frank. Spinning around, the boy ran down the ladder and headed for the gangplank. The two crewmen ran after him.

"Grab that guy!" one shouted as Frank neared the gangplank.

Two guards and several of the crewmen at the rail converged on Frank. He put up such a fierce struggle that it took nearly five minutes to subdue him. When he was finally spread-eagled on the deck, one of the panting guards asked the officer of the watch, "What do we do with him?"

"Keep him here until I find out how he got out

136

of the hold," he replied, then turned to the radio operator. "You'd better get back to the bridge."

He strode off and the radio man went back to his station.

Joe was seated in the radio-operator's chair when the man re-entered the wheelhouse. The operator came to an abrupt halt.

"Who are you?" he asked.

"Joe Hardy."

The radio man regarded him with the wariness of one who suspects he is talking to a madman.

"Are you planning to take over the ship, too?"

"No, I'm just waiting."

"For what?"

"The police. They said they could be here in three minutes." Rising from the chair, Joe went over to peer out the portside window. "There they are now."

A half-dozen cars with blinking roof lights were pulling up in a semicircle around the gangplank. Frantically, the radio operator bolted from the bridge.

For the next twenty minutes, there was complete turmoil. Gang members and crewmen trying to escape down the gangplank were grabbed by the police and whisked into a waiting paddy wagon. Spotlights were turned on those who jumped overboard and attempted to escape by swimming to points farther along the dock. Officers were waiting when the would-be escapees climbed out of the water.

Those who tried to hide aboard the ship were ferreted out by a task force that methodically poked through every nook and cranny from bow to stern.

In the midst of all this chaos, Joe found Frank on deck and the two of them went below to release Chet. When he came up from the hold, he tried to turn along the side passage to the starboard side, but Frank grabbed his arm and asked where he was going.

"To the galley," Chet said. "They didn't bring us any dinner, remember?"

"We'll eat after we finish our business with the police," Frank declared and pulled his reluctant friend the other way.

The officer in charge of the raiding party was Lieutenant Flores, who invited the boys to ride in his car to headquarters. On the way, they discussed the case.

"I met your father in New York last year," the lieutenant said to Frank. "He told me that you two are following in his footsteps."

Joe chuckled. "I'm sure glad you knew who we were. Otherwise you probably wouldn't have believed a word I said!"

"We were suspicious of the *Mary Malone* all along," Lieutenant Flores told him. "Only we had no proof. This uranium caper will enable us to really clean that gang up."

When they reached headquarters, Flores dispatched a raiding party to Devil's Point to arrest the doctor and his two assistants. He also sent a wire to the Atlantic Island police requesting that Captain Sanchez and the desk clerk Lanky at the Atlantic Hotel be arrested. "However," he said to the boys, "I frankly don't expect too much cooperation."

"They'll take off," Frank agreed.

The lieutenant nodded. "We also have an all-points bulletin out for Pete McGinnis, the captain of the *Mary Malone*. He wasn't on board when we raided the ship. Now, I would like you to accompany me and identify the suspects we've arrested."

"We'll be glad to," Frank said.

The boys pointed out Mack Larsoni, the burly foreman, the radio operator, and various other hoods and crewmen, when Joe suddenly realized something. "Ted Herkimer isn't among the prisoners!" he exclaimed.

16 A Grim Chase

Lieutenant Flores was disappointed. "I'll put out an all-points bulletin on him, too," he promised. "Just give me as accurate a description of the man as you can."

The boys did the best they could, then said good-bye to the lieutenant. They went to dinner, where the mystery continued to be the main topic of conversation.

"How do you suppose Herkimer got away?" Chet asked.

"Maybe he wasn't aboard," Joe replied. "Perhaps he was with Captain McGinnis."

"The captain could be the third director," Frank spoke up.

"That's possible," Chet said. "But where are they?"

"If they know the police are after them," Joe suggested, "they'll probably try to get off the island. There are only two ways—by boat or plane. I heard Lieutenant Flores say that he has both the dock and the airport thoroughly covered. So there's nothing much we can do but wait."

"Suppose they phoned Freddie Fredericks on Atlantic Island to come pick them up?" Frank said. "He could swoop down at Pirate's Port Airport just long enough for them to jump on, and take off again before the police know what's happening."

"Maybe we'd better get out there and check," Chet suggested. He looked at his watch. "It's nearly ten PM so they've had over an hour to make plans. And it's only an hour's flight from Atlantic Island to here."

They took a taxi to the airport. There was no sign of the B-24 on the field. Instead of wasting time inquiring at the information desk in the terminal, the boys went directly to the control tower to find out if the plane had been there. They had no trouble getting in when they showed their pilot licenses.

The chief control officer, who introduced himself as Gary Winn, looked at them curiously. "What can I do for you?" he inquired.

"We're private detectives and we're helping the police on a case right now," Frank said. "Has a converted B-24 owned by the Atlantic Island Charter Service landed here in the last couple of hours?"

After checking flight records, Mr. Winn shook his head. "I know the plane you mean. It's owned by a fellow named Freddie Fredericks. He hasn't been around for a couple of days."

"Do you expect him?"

The chief control officer checked a different set of records. "He hasn't filed a flight plan yet," he said.

The boys thanked him and left. Pausing at the bottom of the outside stairs, they discussed their next move.

"Just because he didn't file a flight plan doesn't mean Freddie isn't coming for Herkimer and McGinnis." Joe said. "Maybe he plans to land illegally. This way he could throw off the police in case they're waiting for him."

Frank nodded. "Let's keep an eye on the field for a while."

The young detectives stood for an hour, watching planes land and take off. Finally, Mr. Winn came toward them from the terminal. "Freddie Fredericks just filed a flight plan en route," he told them. "He'll land in ten minutes."

"Can he do that?" Frank asked. "Back home we have to file before we take off."

"We're looser here. There's not so much air traffic.

As long as he informs us that he's coming in, it's legal."

"Thanks for the tip," Frank said. "Would you please call Lieutenant Flores and alert him?"

"Sure will." Gary Winn nodded and went back inside.

The boys watched the field. Soon they saw the landing lights of a plane. It touched down and taxied over to the terminal.

A pilot in goggles and helmet got out, stripped off his head gear, and tossed it back in the cabin. He was Freddie Fredericks!

The boys stayed in the shadows behind him as he went into the terminal and strode toward the first-class lounge.

"He'd spot the three of us tailing him," Frank whispered to Joe and Chet. "I'll follow him while you make yourselves inconspicuous here in the waiting room."

Moments later, Frank peered into the lounge. Several passengers were seated in upholstered chairs. Fredericks looked around as if searching for someone. A tall man dressed in tweeds rose and approached him. Freddie watched him come up, while Frank slipped into the lounge and hid behind a potted palm only a few feet away from the pilot.

"Looking for someone?" the man in tweeds asked Freddie.

The pilot regarded him suspiciously. "Why do you want to know?"

"I thought perhaps you were looking for Ted Herkimer."

Fredericks became even more suspicious. "You're not Herkimer!"

"Didn't say I was. You also looking for Captain Pete McGinnis?"

"You Captain McGinnis?"

"Depends on who you are."

"Let's stop sparring," the pilot declared. "I'm Freddie. Where's Ted?"

"He'll be along. He has to be careful, because the cops have this place blanketed. I would prefer to get out of sight myself."

"Then let's get aboard the plane. Ted can find his way there himself."

The pair walked from the lounge together. Frank followed and watched them walk out the terminal door onto the field. Joe and Chet came over.

"Who's the guy in tweeds?" Joe asked.

"Beats me," Frank said. "He told Freddie he was Captain McGinnis. I think at first he was going to pretend he was Herkimer, but when he found out Freddie knew Ted, he did a smooth switch. They're going aboard the plane and will wait for Herkimer."

Chet said, "There they are!"

145

Ted Herkimer and the *Mary Malone*'s captain were just entering the first-class lounge.

"Let's grab them," Joe said.

"They're probably armed," Frank cautioned. "For once, why don't we be sensible and just point them out to the police?"

"Okay, if you point out the police."

Frank looked around. There wasn't a uniform in sight. "They're probably in plain clothes and we don't know who they are," he said.

They walked over to the first-class lounge and looked in. Herkimer and the captain were standing near the potted palm, fidgeting nervously. Suddenly, Herkimer spotted the boys!

"The Hardys!" he hissed to his companion. "Come on!" The two men broke for the door leading directly onto the field. Frank, Joe, and Chet followed in pursuit. As they ran outside, they saw that the criminals had paused to gaze around wildly for some route of escape. They spotted the B-24 and headed straight for it. The boys sped after them.

Apparently, Freddie saw Herkimer and his companion approaching, because he started up the engines and opened the passenger door. The young detectives were twenty-five yards behind them when Herkimer and Captain McGinnis jumped into the plane and slammed the door shut.

The B-24 began to move. The boys halted, watch-

146

ing in frustration as it taxied toward the runway. Then, unaccountably, the four propellers stopped turning and the aircraft came to a dead stop.

The boys started running again. Joe reached the passenger door first and jerked it open. Ted Herkimer, gripping the doorway on both sides, kicked at him. The young detective grabbed the pilot's foot and pulled him out onto the dirt.

Joe left him for Frank and Chet to handle and jumped into the plane. Frank, seeing Chet could cope by himself, scrambled in after his brother.

Captain McGinnis took a roundhouse swing at Joe. When Joe ducked, the blow caught Frank flush on the jaw. As Frank staggered backward, dazed, Joe landed left and right hooks that put the captain on his back with all the fight knocked out of him.

Joe turned to his brother, who felt his jaw and gave him a reproachful look. Outside, Chet was sitting on Ted Herkimer.

In front of the plane, the man in tweeds was handcuffing the pilot. He held up a badge for the young detective to see.

"You must be the Hardy boys," he said. "Lieutenant Flores told me about you when he alerted me to look for Herkimer and McGinnis. I'm Sergeant Julio Munoz of the airport security police."

17 A Suspect Disappears

Frank smiled. "I'm sure glad to find out you're on our side. We watched you in the lounge and were afraid you were another member of the gang. Did you fix it so the plane wouldn't take off?"

Munoz nodded. "I thought it wouldn't work at all. Then, when it started taxiing, I got plenty worried!" He chuckled, then said, "Hey, how about you fellows helping me take these guys to the airport security office?"

"We'll be glad to." Joe grinned.

The criminals were held at airport security until a paddy wagon arrived. Everyone, including the boys and a uniformed guard, sat in the back. Only the detective rode in front with the driver.

Joe looked at the ship's captain. "Are you the third director of this crazy bunch that wants to rule the world, captain?"

"I don't know what you're talking about," the captain replied.

"What *are* you talking about?" Ted Herkimer asked.

Joe switched his attention to the hatchet-faced man. "Do you know why Dr. Minkovitch wanted that uranium, Ted?"

"What uranium?"

"Aw, come on," Frank put in. "We had Minkovitch's lab bugged and overheard him tell your stooge Larsoni that he was building an A bomb for some liberation movement in Europe. Larsoni must have passed that information on to you."

"I admit nothing," Herkimer said. "But I'm willing to listen to your ramblings."

"Minkovitch was snowing Larsoni. Actually, he has built enough atom bombs to blow up every major city in the world."

"What on earth for?"

"For three people who call themselves directors," Chet spoke up. "They plan to demand complete surrender from every country and want to end up ruling the whole planet."

Herkimer stared at him without comment.

Frank pressed the point further. "We know two of the directors, Lanky and Luis Sanchez, and we have an idea that Pete McGinnis is the third. Do you know if he is?"

Herkimer examined Captain McGinnis as though searching for signs of insanity, then turned back to the boys. "If I'd known any of them were involved in anything like that, I wouldn't have gone within a thousand miles of them. Do you think *I'm* crazy also? Why would I help anybody build bombs that might blow me up, too?"

"I'm certainly not the third director, either," Pete McGinnis spoke up. "I had no idea what was going on."

Freddie Fredericks stared at Herkimer. "If I knew that you guys were this far out, I wouldn't have flown in here!" he ranted. "What a mistake *that* was."

"I'm not involved!" Herkimer said hotly. "I was just in on the hi—" He abruptly cut himself off.

Joe finished the sentence for him. "The hijackings. Which brings us to another subject. Who's the boss of that gang, Ted?"

But Herkimer lapsed into sullen silence.

"You're caught, Ted," Joe went on. "Holding back can't get you anything. Who's the big boss?"

Herkimer emitted a resigned sigh. "All right, it's Cy Ortiz."

"The owner of the trucking company?" Frank said in surprise.

"That's right."

151

"Why would he steal his own stuff?" Chet asked.

"It wasn't his. He just transported it," Herkimer replied.

Frank and Joe were not convinced that Ted was telling the truth, but realized that they had to investigate Ortiz as soon as they got home.

Lieutenant Flores was off duty when they arrived at police headquarters. The boys waited around long enough to see the suspects locked up, then walked to their hotel.

In the morning, they returned to police headquarters. Lieutenant Flores told them that Dr. Minkovitch and his two oversized assistants were in custody, which meant that the police had all of the gang members stationed on Devil's Point.

"The Atlantic Island authorities reported that Lanky and Captain Sanchez couldn't be found," he added.

"While they're really covering up for them!" Frank said grimly.

The lieutenant shrugged. "It's very unfortunate. What are you going to do next?"

"We'll go back to the States and investigate Cy Ortiz," Frank replied.

"I recommend you don't stop at Atlantic Island en route," Flores advised. "You might be taken into custody on some trumped-up charge."

"We won't, lieutenant." Joe grinned. "And thanks for your help."

"I'm indebted to you," the officer replied. "You did me a great favor by delivering evidence against this gang."

The boys caught a shuttle flight to Miami, and from there they took a regular commercial plane to Washington, DC, arriving about seven P.M.

Frank called room twenty-six at the Glasgow Motel and spoke to his father.

"Come on over," Mr. Hardy said. "Stewart Zegas is here with me and he'd like to hear your report."

An hour later, Mr. Zegas said in a tone of satisfaction, "That solves the uranium hijacking. Fenton, can you fly with me to Pirate's Port in the morning?"

"Yes."

"We'll take along someone from the State Department to put pressure on the Atlantic Island police, and a team of nuclear scientists to dismantle Dr. Minkovitch's factory. That should just about close a big portion of the case. Boys, you've done excellent work. In the name of the FBI, I thank you," Mr. Zegas said.

Frank grinned. "I'd feel better if we had our part of the case solved, too. We still have to clean up in Boston."

"Are you flying there in the morning?" Mr. Hardy asked the boys.

"That was our plan," Joe replied.

When the young detectives arrived in Boston the next day, they went directly to the Ortiz Trucking Company warehouse. Their yellow sports sedan was still parked out front.

Cy Ortiz's office was empty. Since it was Saturday, and the warehouse stayed open only a half day, the boys assumed he had gone home early.

They looked for Ox Manley and found the foreman talking to one of the mechanics in the repair garage. He greeted the trio cordially and asked why they had quit after their initial run as backup drivers.

"After being hijacked on the first trip, who wouldn't!" Chet exclaimed.

"Actually, we were curious and did a little investigating," Frank said. "We wanted to find out who's responsible. Some of the information we received seems to indicate that Cy Ortiz is involved in this business."

The foreman looked grim. "In light of something that happened yesterday, I'm sure he is. I didn't understand it at the time, but since you boys mentioned it, I think Ortiz is not only involved but the boss of the hijacking gang!"

"Why?" Joe asked.

"I have to show you something before I explain," Ox told him. "Follow me."

Leading the boys to the storage room, he went

154

to a shelf and took down a small box. It was labeled $\frac{1}{2}''$BOLTS, but a miniature radio speaker was inside.

"Just wait here," Ox said. "I'm going to Ortiz's office."

A minute or so passed, and then his voice came from the small speaker. "Hi, boys. I'm speaking from the boss's office."

A few moments later, he returned and placed the lid on the little box again. "Did you hear me?" he asked.

"We sure did," Frank replied.

"I discovered that by accident," Ox went on. "I was looking for half-inch bolts, and when I opened the carton, I heard Ortiz talking to one of the truckers. He bugged his own office!"

"Why?" Joe asked.

"The only reason I can think of is that the union grievance committee borrows his office for meetings, and he wants to know what they are up to. Anyway, I just happened to overhear a long distance call he got yesterday."

"How could you tell it was a long distance call?" Frank asked.

"The bug is under the desk, right below his telephone. I could hear the operator's voice. It was a person-to-person call from Atlantic Island for Mr. Cy Ortiz."

155

No one said anything for a few moments. Then Joe asked, "Could you hear the conversation?"

"Only Ortiz's side of it. The other guy's voice wasn't as clear as the operator's. I think he was deliberately talking low. I know his name was Lanky, because I heard Ortiz calling him that. He kept saying, 'Oh, Lanky, those blasted Hardy boys.' " He looked questioningly at Frank and Joe. "Do you know who they are?"

"Maybe," Frank said.

"Where's Ortiz now?" Joe asked.

"He walked out right after the conversation and never came back. Obviously, he's run for cover!"

18 A Strange Story

"Maybe he went home," Joe suggested.

"I called his house this morning because I needed some information from him," Ox replied. "His wife hasn't seen him since yesterday."

Frank, Joe, and Chet had the same thought. All the evidence pointed to the fact that Cy Ortiz was, indeed, involved in the gang and perhaps the third director of Lanky's group!

"Did you look for clues in Cy's office?" Frank asked Manley.

"Yes. I found nothing."

"What about the warehouse?" Chet spoke up.

"I wouldn't know where to look or what to look for. Why don't you go and see if you can find some-

157

thing? I just made a thorough inspection of all the trucks in the parking lot, so you can skip them. But maybe something'll turn up in the building."

It was noon, and everyone had left. "I'm going, too, in a few minutes," Manley added. "All you have to do when you're finished is to close the door of the warehouse. It'll lock automatically."

"Okay," Frank said. "And thanks."

The boys started with Cy Ortiz's office. As they went through drawers, Chet asked, "What are we looking for?"

Joe said, "A plane ticket receipt, a memo of his call from Atlantic Island, anything that might indicate where he went."

They found nothing. They made a thorough search of the rest of the downstairs, but again turned up nothing to indicate where Ortiz had gone. They checked loft number one and found it empty. When they came down, they crossed the warehouse to the opposite freight elevator to go up to loft number two.

The elevator rose about six feet and stopped.

Chet pushed the UP button. When nothing happened, he pushed the DOWN button. Again nothing happened. He pushed a red button marked EMER-GENCY and a bell rang on the first floor.

"That won't do any good," Joe said. "There's nobody down there to hear it except mice."

158

Frank said, "If we don't figure some way to get out of here, we're stuck until Monday morning!"

They all looked up at the roof of the car. There was a square vent in it, but it was much too small to climb through.

Chet took a deep breath and let out an ear-splitting Tarzan yell. Frank and Joe grabbed their ears. When the reverberation finally died away, they cautiously dropped their hands.

"What was that for?" Joe asked.

"I hoped somebody outside would hear it."

"Nobody that did would dare come in," Joe said. "He would think there was a gorilla loose."

"Listen," Frank whispered, gazing upward.

The other two looked upward also and listened. There was a slight sound of something metallic scraping against the roof of the car.

"Somebody's up there," Frank whispered.

The end of a rubber hose was poked down through the vent. They couldn't see any vapor coming from it, but a sweetish odor suddenly pervaded the car. They felt a drumming noise in their ears, their sight dimmed, and they had an urge to lie down. They were not alarmed, though. As a matter of fact, they felt a lively sense of well-being. Their arms and legs began to pump as though they were running and they started to laugh uproariously. Then all motion and sound stopped.

159

They awakened in their sports sedan. Frank was slumped over the wheel, Joe leaned against the right front door, and Chet was spread across the back seat. Frank awakened first, reached across and shook Joe. The younger boy's eyes opened gradually, and it was a minute before he became fully oriented. Then he straightened up, looked over his shoulder, reached in back and shook Chet.

Opening his eyes, Chet said, "I'm not going to school today. I'm sick."

Then he realized where he was and sat up.

"What happened?" he inquired.

"We got a dose of nitrous oxide," Frank said. "Otherwise known as laughing gas."

"What's that in your lap?" Joe asked.

Frank looked down and picked up the slip of paper. In block letters was printed: STAY OUT OF MY WARE-HOUSE, HARDY BOYS. GO BACK TO BAYPORT.

Frank held the message for the other two to see. "Cy Ortiz!" Chet exclaimed. "He's still lurking around here."

As the boys climbed from the car, Joe asked, "Now what?"

Frank said, "Ortiz obviously doesn't want us to see something in loft number two. So the next move is to see what it is."

They went back to the warehouse door and found

it locked. Chet said to Joe, "Are there burglar's tools in that detective kit of yours?"

"They aren't necessary," Frank replied. "I still have the key Ortiz gave me."

Taking it out of his pocket, he unlocked the door. "We'd better search the downstairs again before we go up to the loft," he suggested, "just to make sure Ortiz isn't here."

The boys found no one on the first floor, but in the storage room they discovered an empty metal bottle with a hose attached to it. The bottle was labeled: NITROUS OXIDE.

"That's what made that metallic scraping noise on top of the elevator," Frank declared.

This time they were more cautious in using the freight elevator. While Chet and Frank went up, Joe stayed downstairs to go for help in case they got stuck between floors. When the elevator took Frank and Chet up without any trouble, they sent it back down for Joe.

The loft was full of material ready for shipment. There were bales and crates everywhere. The boys moved from pile to pile, reading the labels until Chet suddenly stopped.

"Something's bothering me," he said. "If Ortiz steals this stuff by hijacking his own trucks, doesn't he have to reimburse the owners who ordered him to ship it?"

"He carries insurance," Joe replied. "The insurance company pays off the owners and Ortiz is home free with the loot."

"Oh," Chet said.

They moved on. Suddenly, Joe signaled the others to stop and listen. They could hear furtive footsteps behind a pile of crates.

Joe motioned Chet to go one way, while he and Frank went the other. They rushed around the pile of crates from either side and trapped the intruder, who was trying to reach the elevator. They grabbed him in a flash.

"Hey—take it easy!" the man croaked. He was Dave Falcon, Frank's former driving partner!

The boys released their grip but circled him warily.

"What are you doing here, Dave?" Frank demanded.

"I'd like to ask you the same question!" Falcon shot back.

"Are you working for Cy Ortiz?" Joe asked.

"No, I quit."

"You were working for him, then?" Frank asked.

The Indian looked puzzled. "You know I was. You were my backup."

"I don't mean as a truck driver," Frank said. "I mean as one of his hijack gang."

"Oh, you also know he heads the hijack gang?"

Chet said, "Quit pretending, Falcon. We know you were the guy who gassed us."

The Indian gazed at him with complete lack of understanding.

Frank moved closer. "You'd better tell us what you were doing up here, Dave."

Falcon looked at the three boys and shrugged. "The downstairs door was open, so I sneaked in."

"I didn't ask how you got here, but why."

"I was looking for the cargo hijacked from our truck a few days ago."

Frank said, "What made you think it would be here?"

"Because I thought the masked leader of the hijackers was Ortiz. He held his gun in his left hand, and Ortiz is left-handed."

"Is the cargo here?" Joe asked.

Falcon shook his head. "No."

"Is that why you quit?" Frank asked him. "Because you thought Ortiz was crooked?"

"Well, I didn't really officially quit. Yesterday morning I went into his office to do it, but he wasn't there. Then he jumped me from behind."

"Ortiz jumped you?" Joe asked.

"Let me start from the beginning. When I saw the office was empty, I was about to leave, but then I spotted a note lying on Ortiz's desk. I thought maybe it told where he was and when he would be

163

back, so I picked it up. It was just a memo to himself reminding him to call back somebody named Lanky on Atlantic Island."

The boys looked at each other. The story Ox told them was true!

Dave Falcon continued, "Someone came into the office without making a sound. He got an arm around my neck from behind and squeezed until I blacked out. When I came to, the memo was gone!"

19 *The Masked Ringleader*

"How do you know it was Ortiz?" Frank asked.

"Because it was his left arm that went around my neck. And, as I told you, Ortiz is left-handed!"

Frank and Joe were convinced that the Indian was not lying. Quickly, they explained to him that they were investigating the case and had picked up several clues that tied in with his story.

"I'd like to help," Dave offered. "Maybe we can get to the bottom of this whole thing yet!"

"I can't think of anything you can do right now, Dave," Frank said. "But we may be able to use you later. Where can we get in touch with you?"

The Indian wrote his address and telephone number on a scrap of paper and gave it to Frank. As there was nothing more that could be done until Monday, they went downstairs, locked the building, and left.

The boys checked into a motel. Deciding that they could use some advice from Fenton Hardy, Frank called the Glasgow Motel in Washington. However, the manager told him that Mr. Hardy had checked out. Frank dialed FBI headquarters and found out that his father could be reached at the Corsair Hotel on Pirate's Port.

When Frank phoned Pirate's Port, his father was not there. The boy tried to get in touch with Mr. Hardy several times over the weekend but had no luck. He also contacted the police, who had no clues on Cy Ortiz's disappearance.

On Monday morning, the trio was about to return to the trucking company. "You two go ahead," Frank told Chet and Joe. "I'll try to get Dad once more before I leave."

This time he was lucky and reached his father. After he had explained the situation, Mr. Hardy said, "It seems as if all clues point to Ortiz as the gang leader, but I'd like you to doublecheck on one of them. Find out whether that call from Lanky was really person-to-person for Cy Ortiz."

"Okay, Dad." Frank put down the receiver, then dialed the telephone company. It took some time to get the information he wanted, but when he did, he let out a low whistle. Then he hung up and raced out the door.

When he arrived at the trucking company, Joe and Chet were talking with Ox Manley.

"I have an idea on how we can lure Ortiz out of his hiding place and trap him," the foreman said.

"How?" Frank asked.

"I have a truck going out soon that's loaded with very valuable stereo equipment. I'll spread the word around. Certainly, some of the drivers are in on this hijacking business, and they'll get in touch with Cy. He'll want to take the opportunity and steal the stuff!"

Joe looked skeptically at Frank, remembering Herkimer's words about discontinuing the operation for a while. He was about to say something, when Frank cut him off. "I think that's a wonderful idea," the young detective declared. "Why don't you let *us* drive the truck and—"

Manley grinned. "You're reading my mind, young man. And I'll alert the police. They'll follow you, and when Ortiz and his men attempt to steal the truck—zingo!"

Just then Avery Smithson walked up to the group. "I'm about ready to leave, boss. Do you—"

"Take the day off with full pay," Manley told him. "These two fellows'll drive the truck. And tell Chuck I won't need him, either."

Smithson looked surprised but did not press the point. "Only one thing, boss. Brian Goodman wanted a lift to Washington. Do you think he can still go?"

Manley shrugged. "Sure. Why not?" Then he turned to the boys. "Come on out and I'll show you the rig."

As the group walked to the White truck, Frank excused himself for a moment. He rejoined the group just as Brian Goodman, who was not much older than the Hardys, climbed in the seat next to Joe, who was driving.

Chet held open the back door of the truck. "We get to travel first class," he said to Frank with a grin. "We can stretch out under the sun." With that, he opened the sun-roof panel and the two made themselves comfortable. When they felt the vehicle moving out of the parking lot, Chet looked at his friend.

"I don't get it, Frank. We all overheard Herkimer saying there won't be any more hijackings. Why'd you agree to drive this rig?"

"I have a feeling that our greedy gang won't want to lose all this loot. It's only a hunch I have, but it's worth following up."

Joe and Brian talked about the hijacking and the morale of the drivers, which had sunk to an extremely low point. "Do you think Ortiz may be the cause of it?" Joe asked curiously.

168

"Naw. The boss is an honest man. If he weren't such a decent guy, everyone would've quit by now," Brian replied.

Joe said nothing more on the subject. Neither did he tell Brian why he was driving the rig instead of Avery. *I wish I knew myself,* he thought wistfully. *Why'd Frank ever agree to this? The hijackings are finished and he knows it!*

But they had not driven far when they heard a noise behind them. Brian whirled around and gasped. Joe, at the same time, felt the end of a sawed-off shotgun between his shoulders.

"Get off at the next exit, and then take the second right four miles up to a farmhouse," growled the masked man who had hidden in the cab behind their seats. "And no wrong moves or you're a dead man!"

Joe carefully followed his instructions. At the farmhouse, which was the only dwelling on the road, an International tractor-trailer was waiting for them.

"Back up to its rear door," the gunman said.

Then the man ordered him and Brian out of the cab. Three other masked men were outside and shoved the two into the back of their truck. Joe noticed that the leader held a gun in his left hand and directed his gang with signals rather than commands.

Once locked up in the trailer, Joe stared at his

brother. "I don't believe it!" he said. "Frank, how did you know—"

"I had a feeling the gang wouldn't want to miss out on those stereos. Plus they saw a good chance to get rid of us for good."

Brian's face was ashen. "Would someone tell me what's going on, please?"

"With luck, we'll get the hijackers this time," Frank told him. "The police are behind us."

Soon the boys were ordered out of the trailer and the left-handed leader gestured for them to transfer the cargo from the White to the International trailer.

"There's no point in that," Frank spoke up. "The police are coming any minute."

One of the hijackers snickered. Frank smiled at him, then turned to the leader. "You're holding that gun rather clumsily, Ox. You aren't left-handed. You're merely pretending to be to make everyone think Ortiz is the gang's boss. That's why you used your left arm to choke Dave Falcon."

"Ox Manley!" Chet cried out. "And here we thought—"

Transferring his gun to his right hand, Manley stripped off his ski mask. "Too bad you figured out who I was," he growled. "Now you'll have to take a long ride in a private plane."

"To where?" Chet asked.

"Atlantic Island, where a colleague of mine will

arrange with a certain police captain for all four of you to be put away where you can't talk for the next ten years!"

"I don't think so," Frank said. "You see, I found out that you, not Cy Ortiz, received that cable call from Mr. Lanky the other day. It was clever to plant that fake memo on Cy's desk for the first person who walked into his office to find, then put him out and steal the memo back. That had us fooled for a moment."

Manley laughed nervously. "All that doesn't change the fact that no police are coming, because I never called them."

"Oh, but they're already here," Frank said. "I called them myself just before we got into the truck. By now the entrance to this road is barricaded and you can't go the other way because you're at a dead end!"

20 The Final Clue

The four hoods gazed apprehensively in the direction of the main road. Ox Manley said with an attempt at bravado, "He's trying to panic us, men. No cops are there."

That statement was belied a moment later by a dozen uniformed policemen carrying riot guns who appeared around a curve fifty yards away. Ox Manley and his cohorts bolted for the woods on the right of the farmhouse.

"After them!" Joe cried, racing in pursuit.

Frank and Brian sped after Joe, and Chet lumbered in the rear. The four hoods disappeared into the trees. By the time the boys reached the edge of the woods, they could still hear the pounding feet ahead but could no longer see the fugitives.

Soon the trees began to thin out, however, and the hijackers once again became visible. The boys could hear the pounding feet of the uniformed police far behind them.

Then a road appeared up ahead. Several cars and a school bus lined its sides. As the boys drew nearer, they saw a park with picnic tables beyond it. About thirty children and a few adults were barbecuing chicken. A banner on the side of the school bus read: AVENUE CHURCH SUNDAY SCHOOL PICNIC.

With his three cohorts behind him, Ox Manley ran from one parked car to another, obviously looking for one with the key in the ignition. The boys were twenty-five yards behind when Manley dived into the front seat of a brown sedan. One of the masked bandits got in beside him, and the other two jumped in back. The engine started and the brown sedan's wheels threw gravel as it took off.

The Hardys reached the road with Chet and Brian close behind. All were panting. Like the hoods, they ran along the line of cars, looking inside to see if any had a key in its ignition.

The only one that did was the school bus. As the boys climbed aboard, a stout man wearing a bus driver's cap came running from the picnic area.

Joe slid behind the wheel of the bus. Chet collapsed on the seat behind him. Frank, standing in the doorway, called to the bus driver, "The police will be along to explain."

Joe worked the lever that closed the door and took off along the narrow, roughly graveled road. The bus rocked and shook at each pothole. Frank staggered over and fell into the seat next to Chet.

The speeding car containing the hijackers was engulfed in a cloud of dust ahead. Joe floored the accelerator, increasing the rocking of the bus, but narrowing the distance between it and the getaway car. But the nearer he got, the worse the visibility became because of the dust cloud!

Joe tried to pull ahead of the sedan, but it increased speed as he did, keeping him trapped in the left lane. When he finally managed to pull abreast of the car, they were approaching a curve and rocking like out-of-control broncos.

Then a truck rounded the curve. Joe edged to the right, bouncing the right side of the bus against the sedan's left front fender. Ox Manley lost control and ran into a cornfield. Joe swung into the right lane just in time to avoid a head-on collision with the truck. It went by with its horn blasting.

Joe brought the bus to a stop on the shoulder just short of the curve, switched off the lights, cut the ignition, and removed the keys. The boys jumped out.

The sedan had come to a halt with its wheels buried in loose dirt clear to the hubcaps. Ox Manley and the other three jumped out and ran toward the bus with leveled guns.

"Step aside!" Ox shouted. "We're going to take that bus."

"Be my guest!" Joe said and threw the keys in a long arc over the cornfield.

Ox Manley screamed in frustration. "Now why did you do that?"

Joe grinned as three cars came from the direction of the picnic area. They pulled behind the bus and a number of policemen poured out.

"Throw down your weapons," the sergeant in charge commanded as he and his men covered the hijackers with riot guns.

When the ski masks of Manley's cohorts were pulled off, the Hardys recognized the men as the ones they had seen in the Chesapeake Bay cottage with Ted Herkimer. Later they had piloted the stolen Spectrocolor TV sets to the *Mary Malone*.

The police drove the criminals away in the three cars. It took the boys a while to find the key to the bus, and then they used the large vehicle to pull the brown sedan from the cornfield. When they got back to the picnic area with Frank driving the sedan, they gave the bus driver and the owner of the sedan their addresses, but both told them the police had promised to take care of any necessary repairs.

"Do you think our rig is still by that farmhouse?" Brian asked.

Joe grinned. "I suppose so. Who else would want it?"

"Are you driving it to Washington?"

Frank looked concerned. "We've got to find Cy Ortiz," he said.

"That's fine with me," Brian said. "I'll be glad to take the cargo."

"Thanks, Brian. That'll be great. We'll catch a train back to Boston," said Frank.

It was dark when the boys got back to the warehouse. They climbed into their sports sedan and drove to police headquarters.

The sergeant who had brought in Ox Manley and his men told them that the four had been booked but were not talking. Frank and Joe asked to see Manley and were led to his cell, but when they questioned him about Cy Ortiz, he remained silent and refused to even look at them.

When the Hardys reached their motel, they found a message to call their father. Mr. Hardy sounded cheerful. "I want you to know that everything is cleared up at this end," he said. "Dr. Minkovitch's factory has been dismantled, and the uranium is en route to the United States. Our State Department put much pressure on the Atlantic Island authorities, and it seems they managed to find your friend Mr. Lanky. He's in custody now."

"Great," Frank said. "What about Captain Sanchez?"

"He's been suspended and is under investigation for accepting bribes and for conspiracy as one of the directors. He admitted that the third director was Ox Manley."

"We've pretty well cleaned things up here, too," Frank said. "Manley also turned out to be the hijack ringleader and is in jail. The only remaining loose end is that Cy Ortiz is still missing."

"Manley must be responsible for that," Mr. Hardy said. "Can't the police get him to talk?"

"Not so far. And he won't even look at us, let alone answer questions."

"Well, I hope you locate Ortiz soon," the private detective said. "I'll be flying home tomorrow. See you in Bayport."

"All right, Dad. Good-bye."

When he hung up, Frank said in a disappointed voice, "I was hoping that Dad could give us some sort of tip on how to find Ortiz."

Chet said, "I just had a brilliant idea. A clue's been staring us in the face all along and we missed it."

"What?" Joe and Frank asked together.

"Remember when Ox Manley suggested that we check the warehouse? He said we didn't have to bother with the trucks in the parking lot, because he had just given all of them a thorough inspection."

"That's right!" Frank exclaimed. "Let's go!"

They ran out to the car and jumped in, with Frank behind the wheel. He kept the speed limit all the way to the warehouse.

The parking lot gate was locked, but Frank pulled the sports sedan in close to it and they climbed over from the roof of the car.

"No one's likely to be hidden in the trucks that are used every day," Joe said. "My guess is that if Cy is here at all, he'll be in one of the grounded ones awaiting repairs."

Frank nodded. "Let's try the three over by the garage first."

The trucks he was referring to stood in the most isolated part of the lot. As the boys approached, they heard a muffled banging coming from the middle one. Quickly, Frank unlatched and opened the trailer door and shone his flashlight inside.

On the floor, bound hand and foot and gagged, lay Cy Ortiz! He had managed to wriggle on his back near enough to the side of the trailer to kick it with his feet.

179

Quickly, they took off his gag and untied him. Joe ran to the warehouse to get some water, and, after a few moments, the trucking company owner was able to speak.

"I—I'm so glad you found me," he said.

"Were you tied up in this truck all along?" Frank asked him.

Ortiz stretched his aching limbs. "Yes. Ox Manley and his gang came every night to feed me and let me wash up in the rest room of the warehouse, but otherwise I've been here for days. Manley did it because I found out he was the head of the hijack gang."

"We know," Frank said. "He and his gang are in jail."

Ortiz was flabbergasted when he heard what had happened. "It's a good thing that you boys solved the mystery," he said finally. "Do you realize that you prevented a terrible disaster? If these crazy guys had gotten away with their scheme, the results would have been too horrible to contemplate!"

The next morning, en route to Bayport, Chet said, "You know Mr. Ortiz was right. We just saved the world. And I must say, I've had enough adventure for a while. Could we try to stay out of trouble for the next couple of months?"

"I would like nothing better," Frank agreed.

"Holding my thumb on that atom bomb lever is going to give me nightmares for years!"

None of them knew that shortly after they got back home, they would be helping a college football star in *Game Plan for Disaster*.

JOIN NANCY DREW
AT THE COUNTRY CLUB!

You can be a charter member of Nancy Drew's River Heights Country Club™— Join today! Be a part of the wonderful, exciting and adventurous world of River Heights, USA™.

You'll get four issues of the Country Club's quarterly newsletter with valuable advice from the nation's top experts on make-up, fashion, dating, romance, and how to take charge and plan your future. Plus, you'll get a complete River Heights, USA, Country Club™ membership kit containing an official ID card for your wallet, an 8-inch full color iron-on transfer, a laminated bookmark, 25 sticker seals, and a beautiful enamel pin of the Country Club logo.

It's a retail value of over $12. But, as a charter member, right now you can get in on the action for only $5.00. So, fill out and mail the coupon and a check or money order now. *Please do not send cash.* Then get ready for the most exciting adventure of your life!

— —

MAIL TO: Nancy Drew's River Heights Country Club
House of Hibbert   CN-4609
Trenton, NJ 08650

Here's my check or money order for $5.00! I want to be a charter member of the exciting new Nancy Drew's River Heights, USA Country Club™.

Name _____ Age _____

Address _____

City _____ State _____ ZIP _____

Allow six to eight weeks for delivery.   NDDC6

157